The Fairy Tale Whisperer

A Zimbell House Anthology

The Fairy Tale Whisperer

A Zimbell House Anthology

For permission requests, write to the publisher at the address below:
"Attention: Permissions Coordinator"
Zimbell House Publishing, LLC
PO Box 1172
Union Lake, Michigan 48387
www.ZimbellHousePublishing.com

© 2015 Zimbell House Publishing, LLC
Cover Design by The Book Planners
www.TheBookPlanners.com

Published by Zimbell House Publishing, LLC
www.ZimbellHousePublishing.com
All Rights Reserved

Print ISBN: 978-1-942818-00-7
Kindle ISBN: 978-1-942818-01-4
Digital ISBN: 978-1-942818-267
Trade Paper ISBN: 978-1-945967-38-2
Library of Congress Control Number: 2015900602

First Edition: January/2015
10 9 8 7 6 5 4

The Fairy Tale Whisperer is a collection of some of our favorite fables told from the prospective of perhaps a bit jaded, a tad older, and sometimes wiser characters.

Zimbell House Publishing is pleased to be showcasing the talents of twelve emerging writers that we are sure you will enjoy. These contest submissions are presented as submitted without content editing.

Zimbell House Publishing is proud to acknowledge the following contest winners:

Allison Hadley for *Climbing Up the Rabbit Hole*
~ First Prize Winner

Katherine Hannula Hill for *Ella*
~ Second Prize Winner

Kathleen Murphy for *Ruby and Romulus*
~ Third Prize Winner

Acknowledgements

The production of this anthology could not be accomplished without the dedication and literary expertise of our Zimbell House team.

Our sincere thanks goes out to everyone who submitted for this anthology, for without you, there would be no new voices to tempt us.

Zimbell House would like to thank The Book Planners for another great cover design.

Contents

Inspired By

Alice in Wonderland

Bunny

By Kate Harrad

In Mr. WR's living room there were two chairs and a chest of drawers. There were bookshelves covering every wall and layers of crumpled old papers across the floor. Mr. WR crawled across the floor, searching.

He had nobody to speak to, but still he spoke. "Oh dear," he said to nobody. "My mind these days is like one of those rooms stuffed to the very brim with cushions and books and those little side tables and what is it rooms are stuffed with? Oh yes," he glanced down, "old papers. Too full ever to be able to find anything. Time to put a lit match in the middle of it all and let it burn to emptiness. Except I can't find any matches."

He sat down.

"It's just, if I can't find the invitation I won't know when she's coming. And I have to prepare for her arrival. There must be cake. And little jam tarts. Will she want little jam tarts? Or did she ban them? Oh dear, there was an edict here somewhere, it's so hard to keep track, I know she banned some form of pastry… was it croissants? No, why would she ban croissants? It was jam tarts, I'm sure of it."

Musing, he caught sight of himself in the one small mirror.

"Oh my beard! My whiskers! I must trim – but then I'd have to find my razor, and we're back to the same problem all over again. I'm sure I only trimmed them last week. Time's getting away from me, escaping, slipping between my fingers. I'm too weak to hold it, too old. Time's so much stronger than me."

He made a brief ineffectual attempt to look for a razor and gave up.

"I used to know someone who knew time," he reflected. "He talked about it as if it were an angry god. He thought he'd been cursed by time. Perhaps he had. Perhaps I have. It's waiting in the wings-"

He looked anxiously into all five corners of the room, just in case.

"But no, time has certainly passed for me, as it's supposed to. It stopped for him, though, my poor mad friend. No more time for you. All dead, all of them, so long ago. Just me left. Me and her. Oh my beard... oh, where is that invitation? She'll be so angry – but she's always angry. If only I could say no to her invitations. But she wouldn't like that.

"It used to be threats, when she was angry. Before the thing with the girl, I mean. She'd shout, but you could pacify her - her husband could, anyway, sometimes. We laughed at her sometimes, the king and I, although only when she was definitely a long way away and couldn't hear us. All sound and fury we said. But she did signify something.

"After the girl, it wasn't just threats any more. It was heads, rolling like dice. Like round dice. Round dice with mouths open in shock, and no winning for anyone. Once she'd been mocked to her face, the land wasn't a safe place to live. The girl ruined it all.

"And the king, my friend, was the first to go. A diffident man, a man lacking in confidence, but that was a bond between us. I've never had any confidence. My wife had confidence for both of us. She knew what to do. She would have been able to tell me where the razor is, where the invitation is.

"Perhaps I had better just admit that I can't find it. And I can't remember when she said she was going to visit. Why does she write her own invitations when she visits me? I would have written one if she'd told me to. I would have had it engraved on gold paper, in gold ink – no, wait, that wouldn't have worked – black ink on gold paper, perhaps. With curlicues. I'm not sure what they are but I expect she would want them. Had it delivered by heralds with trumpets, 'To Her Most Divine Majesty, the Queen of our Hearts, from her humble servant Mr. WR, an invitation to tea'… well, I wouldn't have been able to afford proper heralds or trumpets but I know a tramp who owes me a favor and has had a couple of bagpipe lessons. But no, she has to control everything.

"Or was she protecting me? I would have been bound to get a word wrong or missed one of her titles, and then she'd have had me ex-

"—so perhaps it's a good sign. She doesn't want me to do something wrong because she doesn't want to lose me. Perhaps she's visiting to apologize for – no, of course not, what am I saying? Anyway, the point is, I have to be prepared at all times, from now onwards. A fresh pot of tea always waiting, some form of non-banned teatime snack in the cupboard, and I should probably tidy."

The thought itself was exhausting; he collapsed under its weight, back on to the paper-strewn floor.

"As if that's going to happen. I stopped tidying years ago and I'm too old to start again now. Anything could be living under the clutter, I'm sure I saw a small colony of dormice the other day, I think they may actually own the deeds to the house now. Oh my beard…"

From outside there was clamor. Mr. WR gave a violent twitch.

"Oh, will you stop it!" said a voice. "Go on, stand back, stay outside. I can knock on a door without my fingers falling off."

Knock. Knock.

"Oh my-! Oh my-! Oh my-!" Mr. WR scurried to open the door. "Your Majesty! Your Majesty! Such an honor, such an honor, do come in, do come in-"

"Really, Mr. WR, must you say everything twice?" said the Queen, making her way with some care through the floor's debris. "It's a perfect waste of words. There are children who don't have enough words, you know. You should consider making a donation."

"Sorry, Ma'am" Mr. WR opened his mouth to continue apologizing, paused, reconsidered, and closed it again.

"Much better. Now, where is my tea?"

"It'll be ready any minute, ma'am. The truth is – well, I—"

"You lost my note inviting myself to tea and couldn't remember when I was arriving."

"Yes, Ma'am."

"You probably don't even have any tea in the house."

"Well, not as such– I have a lot of pieces of paper-"

"And I wouldn't be surprised if you had some jam tarts tucked away in one of these cupboards, despite my outlawing them a full three years ago."

"No, ma'am, I would never-"

"You're getting old, Mr. WR. You're forgetting things."

"I am, ma'am. I'm so sorry, I'll - punish myself in some way-"

"Don't panic, it's annoying. And I'm sad to see how little you think of me."

"Er… ma'am?"

The Queen smiled. "What kind of monarch blames her subjects for reaching old age? Heaven knows few enough of them have been allowed to. It's quite a novelty for me."

"Er – yes, ma'am."

"How many years have we known each other?"

"A long time, ma'am."

"We've outlived all the others, haven't we?"

"Yes, ma'am."

"There are bonds between us that can never fade. Didn't I have your wife killed?"

There was a pause.

"Yes, ma'am, you did."

"I thought so. I didn't like the way she looked at me."

"She was blind, ma'am."

"Are you offering that as an excuse?"

"No, ma'am."

"Anyway, what right did she have to be blind?"

"You had her blinded, ma'am."

"Did I? I'm sure there was a reason. Maybe it was because I didn't like the way she looked at me. You see, everything I do makes sense if you think about it for long enough in the right way. It's just that so few people can think logically."

Mr. WR was silent.

"Well, if there really isn't any tea I won't stay. I just wanted to ask you something."

He recovered himself. "Of course, ma'am."

"Have you heard of the Dreamers?"

"I… I don't think so, no, ma'am, doesn't ring a bell, doesn't sound familiar…"

"Nobody's visited you recently to discuss… dreams?"

"Nobody's visited me for years, Your Majesty. I thought you – that is, my understanding was that-"

"That you're under house arrest and have been since the death of your wife? Yes, of course you have, but these people are cunning. They may have sneaked in when my guards were busy playing cards. I know they do it. Or one of the guards might be a Dreamer. I've had to execute several already on suspicion. But nobody's come to see you?"

"No, I swear-"

"Interesting."

"Ma'am?"

"Last month I captured one of them alive. She talked, eventually. She was the granddaughter of the hatter. Do you remember your friend the hatter?"

"I was just thinking about him earlier, actually."

"Strange little man. I would have left him alone if only he hadn't been involved in you-know-what. But he was, and I had him disposed of, and apparently it caused some resentment amongst his family. People are so petty. So she joined this group, this underground organization. This *conspiracy*."

"There's a conspiracy against you, ma'am?"

"So it would seem."

"I didn't know that."

"Well, in that case my guards *have* done their job after all. I'm surprised. Do you know you're something of a celebrity out there?"

"Only because you've left me alive."

"Well, that warrants celebrity status, doesn't it? You're the only surviving witness of the incident with – the girl. People wonder why I've let you live."

It was hard to sit still. Mr. WR began to wander round the room, looking at shelves and in drawers.

"I have wondered that myself, ma'am. Especially after what you did to my – I mean, aren't you afraid I harbor resentment? Aren't you afraid I'll remind people about what happened with the girl?"

"Oh my dear man, as if you could be a threat. Look at you. I could have you tortured and you'd thank me. It's easy enough to keep you alive, just to remind people how merciful I can be.

"And perhaps I want a reminder, occasionally, of the girl. Especially now when she's become a symbol to this rebel group. Do you know what you, and she, and they, and your late wife, remind me of? How *powerful* I am."

Mr. WR gave a sigh. He picked something out of a drawer and turned back, towards the Queen.

"You shouldn't have told me," he said quietly, "about the rebels. It gave me hope. I haven't had hope for so many years. Perhaps Alice was right."

"Don't you dare mention her name!" shouted the Queen. "Guards!"

"I blamed her, but the problem wasn't that she mocked you." He came closer. "It's that we didn't. My wife, dead. My friends, dead. My country, terrified. All because we let you take yourself seriously. And now that I have hope that this long nightmare may be ending, that time may have forgiven us for our mistake, I have remembered something."

She looked up at him, contemptuous. "What?

He came up behind her and put his hand to her throat.

"I have remembered - *ma'am* - where my razor is."

Climbing Up the

Rabbit Hole

By Allison Hadley

"Do you know why you're here, Alice?" the curly, dark-haired woman asks with her glasses sitting at the tip of her nose. I like it when that happens. It reminds me of the librarian when I was a child. Oh, those were my favorite. Those summer days rushing to my favorite reading tree after a trip to the library. It was an elm, I remember. And sometimes ants would crawl up into the books and I had to flick them off with my finger.

"Alice, are you listening to me?" the woman says, this time leaning forward with a frown. Crossing her arms and scowling, the long, blonde-haired young lady decides to reply.

"Of course I am, Dr. Fairbanks. My mind was just wandering," Alice says. The doctor sighs and writes on a piece of paper on the desk. I don't see why she's the one being all impatient. I've been here for three days now, getting asked the same questions over and over again.

"I'm here because everyone thinks I'm crazy."

"We don't use that word around here. Now, I know you think you're-"

"No, actually, I don't. I think I'm quite sane," Alice interrupts with her nose held up into the air. And now she prattles on again. Doesn't she know I have someplace to be? I'm sure they have started the party by now, and I'm missing all the fun. The singing, the cake, the tea. . . I can see it now. But the only thing Alice can really see is the Rabbit's shadow frantically hopping around her chair.

"... if you don't talk to me, I will not be able to help you," the doctor says in exasperation. Alice's eyes grow double in size.

"You wish to help me?" she asks.

"Why, yes, Alice. Of course!" Dr. Fairbanks says with a reassuring smile. Alice's face brightens. She sits straight up and claps her hands.

"Wonderful! I need to get out of here. I fear I'm dreadfully late already."

"Late for what?" the doctor inquires.

"The tea party, with the Hatter and Hare. They're going to be performing a new rendition of 'The Walrus and the Carpenter' for me," Alice proclaims proudly. The doctor furrows her brow, the way one makes when they are utterly confused.

"Who are the Hatter and Hare? And what's the occasion?"

"They're friends of mine. They think it's my birthday. I've told them before it's not, but they go on about how they must celebrate. I haven't the heart to correct them again. You see, they're quite mad. It used to bother me, but in a way, it's kind of endearing. And besides, we all need a celebration for ourselves once in awhile! Don't you agree, Dr. Fairbanks?" Alice asks gleefully.

"Yes, indeed I do," the doctor replies hesitantly. Slowly writing on the paper again, she continues, "How did you meet them? And why do they call him, I presume, Hare?" Alice throws her hair back and laughs before she responds.

"Because he's a Hare, silly! I met them in Wonderland when I was still a girl. I haven't been there in far too long. We really should get going. I don't want them to think I won't be attending." Alice begins to stand up from her seat.

"Please, Alice, sit down. We have more to discuss," Dr. Fairbanks pleads. She takes a deep breath and holds it for several seconds before exhaling. "Besides, I don't know how to get to Wonderland. Is it out of the country?" Alice sits back down and straightens the blue hospital gown over her knees.

"I don't know, really. I usually get there by rabbit hole," she says in a matter-of-fact tone. Dr. Fairbanks nods while examining the young woman's face. She writes on the paperwork again, then returns her gaze to Alice.

"Is that why you jumped out that window?" she asks. Alice frowns.

"I never jumped out a window."

"But you did, just five days ago."

"No, I didn't. I leapt into a rabbit hole, but it must not have been one, since I'm here. And it was only three days ago," Alice argues stubbornly. Dr. Fairbanks pages through her paperwork.

"Five days ago. That is what it says here in your chart. You spent two days at the general hospital to confirm you received no critical injuries, and transferred here after they decided no worse injuries were sustained. So, you were leaping into what you thought was a rabbit hole?"

Huh, that's strange. The Hatter must have spoken to Time for me! So for me, it's only been three days but for everyone else it has been five. Does that mean I have lost two days, or have they? I suppose it doesn't matter much, as long as I attend the party on time. Oh what is she muttering to herself about now? Reports, consistency, histories...   that reminds me, I must have missed that history exam! The professor will not be happy with me. Well, it's no matter now. I have other things to concern myself with.

"Alice, I don't have much time left so I need to start wrapping this up for the day. The nurses tell me you have been refusing to take the medication?"

"Yes. They won't make me any smaller, and that's what I need right now."

"To get down the rabbit hole."

"Of course."

"Yes, of course," Dr. Fairbanks says with a flat expression. She takes a few moments to write more notes into the chart.

"Well, Alice, I do strongly advise you to take the medication. It likely won't make you smaller, but it should help. We'll talk again tomorrow. I appreciate the conversation being less one-sided this time."

But...   I need to leave. Alice hits her fist against the chair's armrest and gets up from her seat in a fitful flurry. She returns to her room, where she stares out the window looking to find the right hole. It must be nearby if the Rabbit is here. I'll tell him to inform the party about my tardiness, maybe then it won't be as entirely rude. She sits at her window the rest of the day until the evening, when she dreams of delicious tarts and silly songs.

The following day, Dr. Fairbanks guides Alice into the room, where she crosses her arms and sits on a dark red leather seat. Dr. Fairbanks opens her chart and quickly scans it. She takes a short sigh and looks up at Alice. She pushes her glasses up her nose.

"Still didn't take your medication today?"

"I already told you. They won't do what I need them to do," Alice says with a pout. Dr. Fairbanks stares at her while lightly tapping her pen on the desk.

"I spoke with your sister this morning," she declares. Alice's eyes shoot up from the floor to the doctor, as wide as a doe's after seeing the huntsman.

"Why would you do that?! I haven't spoken to her in ages!" she shouts out in panic.

"She had called me. Your flat mate spoke to her last night. She was very worried about you and wanted to know how you are doing," the doctor says reassuringly. Alice's jaw clenches for a moment, then she leans forward quickly as her hands grip the doctor's desk.

"You didn't tell her anything, did you?" *Please, say no... she just doesn't understand.* Dr. Fairbanks swallows and carefully reads over the very first documents from the file.

"When you were admitted, you gave consent. Your flat mate said your sister is the only one in your family you still speak to on occasion. You signed the paperwork, so yes, I updated her," the doctor says firmly, masking the worry inside. Alice stares into the doctor's eyes, examining, hoping she'll say something else. When the doctor says nothing more, Alice dramatically throws herself back into the chair.

"She gave me some interesting information, Alice," Dr. Fairbanks remarks in an inquisitive tone. Alice's eyes remain fixated on a far off place. "She told me you spoke of Wonderland to her once before when you were both children. You had run up to her from inside the house, sat next to her while she was reading and complained there were no pictures in her book. She said then you disappeared for the day. When they found you, you were covered in grass and brush out in a park. Your Mom left your Dad shortly after that event. Your sister said you spoke of Wonderland for at least a year after it. Alice, can you tell me what happened that day?"

Alice moves her eyes back to the doctor without changing her position, one arm over her forehead and the other hanging heavily, lazily over the armrest of the chair.

"Well, I started following a white rabbit. He had been wearing a waistcoat and pocket watch, which I found quite strange-"

"No, Alice," the doctor interrupts. "I meant what happened before you saw your sister by the tree." She turns her eyes away from the doctor and tightly crosses her arms over her chest.

"Nothing," Alice replies curtly. The doctor searches the young woman's face with a skeptical brow.

"I'm afraid that's not what your sister said. Your mother had told her that-"

"What she said is absolute nonsense!" Alice shouts in interruption, eyes glaring at Dr. Fairbanks. Her brows raise in surprise at the outrage before her. Defeated, she sighs and softly closes the chart.

"Alright. I can see you don't want to talk about this right now. But please, let me help you. And please, help yourself! Take the medication. Your flat mate brought you clothes. Take a shower. Put them on. Go into the common room and talk with people."

"I don't want to talk to them. They're all off their rockers," Alice mumbles.

"I've told you before. We don't use terms like that here. Consider what I've said, Alice. I'll see you tomorrow."

But Dr. Fairbanks didn't see her. Alice refused to see her that day. She refused to take the medication, too. She spent the day talking with the Rabbit, singing with the Tortoise and from the window searching for rabbit holes and doors that would take her back to Wonderland. At night, she spoke with the Cheshire Cat about taking the medication. After discussing at great length both the pros and cons, Alice promised the Cat she would take the medication the next day.

She did. She did not grow smaller like she had hoped. The Cat said maybe it would the following day. Alice still refused to see Dr. Fairbanks. She was very upset with her for thinking she was mad and talking to her sister. The day after, Alice took the medication but continued to decline seeing the doctor. To her dismay, she did not get any smaller nor any taller. Her Wonderland friends were not conversing as much as they had been. She was not pleased about it. The next day, Alice was about to refuse the medication until the Cat encouraged her to take it again. It was the last time she saw the Cheshire that day. She could only catch glimpses of the Rabbit's frantic hopping, and was disappointed to discover the Queen of Heart's marching court out the window was simply a group of nurses walking out for a cigarette. She spent the remainder of the afternoon and evening paging through month old magazines and napping. But, maybe things will start changing for Alice the following day.

The nurse leaves Alice's room after she swallows her medication down hard. I know I won't get any smaller. I know I won't ever. Holding her breath, she waits for the Rabbit to greet her. Alice sadly sighs. I doubt I'll see the Tortoise today, too. She eyes the bag containing the clothes her flat mate brought her. She had packed Alice's favorite blue jeans and light yellow empire-waist top with a white lace bib, in addition to other staples of her wardrobe. Next to the bag sits a plastic bucket full of hygiene products the hospital provided her. Alice grabs the plastic bucket and enters the bathroom.

Steam encircles her as she takes a hot shower. After rinsing her hair, she watches the steam, imagining the pictures she once saw in the Caterpillar's smoke. A nostalgic smile crosses her lips as tears well up in her eyes. "I shall never seem them again," she says to herself. With those words, she lets out a sob. She weeps the hardest and longest she has in quite some time. I should stop. I'll drown in my tears. Alice opens her eyes and allows herself a breath, for she knows that is not true. She watches little rivers turn into whirlpools at the bottom of the shower floor. As another wave of tears hit her, she crosses her arms across her breasts and gently rests her head against the shower's wall. She lets it all go, trusting the drain to wash her lamentations away.

Alice buttons up a blue cardigan after slipping into blue and cream-striped pajama pants. She runs her fingers through her hair as she approaches her room's window. She stops just as she passes the bed. Alice turns around, walks to her belongings bag and rummages through it. She pulls out an historical romance book her flat mate bought for her. Softly, she sits down on the bed. Day turns into night as she gently turns the pages, until eventually she falls asleep.

Alice finishes brushing her wet locks and takes in the morning sun when the nurse opens her door. "Shall I send the doctor away again, Miss?"

Alice runs her fingers on the edge of the curtain, feeling every stitch of the hem. "No, please don't," she replies while turning to the nurse. "I'll see Dr. Fairbanks today."

The nurse gives a proud, tight-lipped smile as she closes the door. Alice starts for the mirror, where she examines herself with fresh eyes. She carefully touches the reflection of her cheek, fingers trembling as they get closer. They press softly against the silver surface. She gives herself a half-smile, then straightens her yellow top before leaving her room.

When Alice enters the room, she lowers her eyes. Dr. Fairbanks glances up. The sight of a bathed, regularly-clothed Alice surprises her. The sight gives her hope.

"It's good to see you again," Dr. Fairbanks says with a soft smile. Alice settles herself into the dark red leather chair. "According to the nurses, you have been taking your medication for four days now."

Alice half smiles and turns her head. "Yes, but it hasn't made me any smaller, as you can see."

Dr. Fairbanks lets out a chuckle. "Indeed. Anything else? Any side effects?"

"I haven't seen the Rabbit today. I haven't really seen any of them. Just quick, faint shadows, it seems. And they don't talk to me anymore."

The doctor nods and quickly jots notes into the chart. "You sound a little disappointed."

"I am," Alice replies. She runs her fingertips over the scratches up and down her arms. "Dr. Fairbanks, I jumped out of a window. How am I still alive? How do I have no broken bones?"

The doctor stops her writing and looks up at Alice, glasses slipping to the tip of her nose. "Well," she answers while straightening them, "it was only a second-story window. There were quite a few rose bushes that broke your fall. It's why you have plenty of scratches instead of fractures."

Alice nods and catches herself picking at the scabs. She stops herself mid-scratch, then takes a deep breath. "That day I jumped, I saw my Dad on campus. I don't know how he found me. He apologized, said he wants to be back in my life again. I called him the Jabberwock, and ran away. He shouted that he's not going to give up on me yet. I didn't know what to do."

"The Jabberwock?" Dr. Fairbanks asks with furrowed brow.

"A monster," Alice patiently answers, "from Wonderland. Anyway, I didn't want to deal with it. When I got home, I saw my flat mate had left her alcohol out on the table. I drank half of something, hoping it'd make me smaller, and ran over to the window. I figured I'd end up in Wonderland again, or maybe somewhere else. I figured anywhere would be better than here."

The doctor nods slowly. Alice slumps her shoulders forward with a pained expression on her face. She looks the doctor in her eyes.

"I really went there, you know, when I was a kid," Alice declares.

"I believe that you truly believe that," Dr. Fairbanks concedes with a half-smile. Alice rolls her eyes. The doctor rests her head on her palm. "Look, I understand you had something terrible happen to you when you were just a child. And I can imagine how seeing your father again could trigger all that. However there are legal outlets you can take to keeping him away from you. But jumping out of a window. Tell me, how has running away helped you?"

"I had an adventure outside of this world," Alice responds quietly, as though lost in a dream. Dr. Fairbanks puts down her pen and clasps both her hands over the chart. She waits until Alice's gaze returns to her own, which takes several moments.

"I can see how running, or in your case leaping, away from the world sounds appealing, considering it seems like an awful place after some of the things your sister said you have experienced. But Alice, this world can be a wonderland too, if you only open your eyes to it."

Alice cries in silence. Finally, she wipes her eyes and nods with a sniffle. The doctor hands her a tissue box. She asks Alice questions regarding side effects and discharging. Alice responds quietly yet with a fragile confidence.

"I'll see you again tomorrow?" Dr. Fairbanks asks. Standing up from her seat, Alice nods and wipes her eyes again with a tissue. The doctor smiles and writes in her notes as Alice exits the room.

Habitually, she begins walking to her own room when from the corner of her eye she sees a shadow. She stops to peer into the common room, where the shadow caught her attention. Five people sit in it, some staring off, another working on a puzzle and two more paging through a magazine while talking. Oh, which way should I go? Alice takes a step toward the common room. Maybe they will have tea in there. The shadow meanders around the room.

The man and woman staring off, both in green hospital gowns, pay no mind when Alice walks into the common area. The red-headed lady in a gray hooded pullover looks up to examine her, then turns her attention back to the puzzle. The two with the magazine, a young man in a football jersey and a young lady in a black T-shirt, both smile when Alice approaches them.

"Hey, I'm Derek and this is Fiona," the young man says. The young lady waves. "What are you in for?"

Alice grimaces and turns to sit at another table when she notices the shadow again. Perched over Derek's shoulders, it materializes as the Cheshire. It smiles and cocks its head toward the duo.

"C'mon, you can tell us," Fiona says with a warm smile.

"Yeah," Derek chimes in. "Besides, we're all crazy here!"

The Cheshire Cat smiles even larger. Starting from its tail, it begins disappearing until all that remains is its white smile. Then that, too, vanishes within the blink of an eye. Alice smiles wistfully, then pulls out a chair across from the duo.

"I'm Alice," she says quietly.

"It's nice to meet you," they say happily. Fiona asks Alice if she'd like some tea, to which Alice gratefully accepts. The three talk about comics, stories, their favorite childhood games. They play charades, discuss why they all are there, what each other have seen and heard. Sometimes they speak of nonsensical things, which make them all burst into laughter. They play, laugh, cry and simply enjoy each other's company until it is time for bed.

When Alice lays down that night, she glimpses the crescent moon outside the window.

Reminded of the Cheshire, she grins and closes her eyes. "Goodnight, Wonderland," she whispers. Within moments, she slips off into dreamland, trusting in the morning she will awake into a new world she has been running from since she was a girl.

Inspired By

Snow White

Dwarves-Idols

By Darlena Cunha

From the first day I arrived in the castle, the mirror in my chamber played tricks on me.

One day it would show me as intensely beautiful, a perfect version of myself. The next it would show me aged and gnarled with a hooked nose, a wrinkled brow. After a particularly grotesque image of myself covered in blood, I grabbed a candlestick and made to smash the mirror. That's when it began to tell me the story of Snow White. What had passed, what was happening then, and what was to come. I never breathed a word of it to anyone, something I regret now, as you guards take me away, shaking your heads in pity and disgust.

The mirror told me that as Snow White grew from a toddler into a young girl, a band of men who called themselves the dwarfs would tempt her from her home, would trick her far into the forest to a cottage and make her their prisoner. They would force her to clean their little cabin in the woods, cook for them, and lay in their beds, as soon as she was of childbearing age.

It told me that I was already in the grip of this spell, that my coming to the castle was part of the plan, and that

I would take the fall for their treachery. I thought I could outwit them, and said as much…it was the only time I ever spoke to that wretched looking glass. The thing simply laughed and bubbled up an image of my lover, shocking me into silence, and sending my efforts underground. Little did I know that that was also part of the plan. Tricky, those dwarfs, very tricky.

As Snow White grew older, she wandered off toward the forest more and more. I forbade her to enter. Her father thought it was because I wanted her to grow up to be a proper young lady, and he overruled me, granting her permission behind my back.

I had a huntsman start following her at a distance. I wanted to know where she was and whether or not the dwarfs were bothering her.

This worked for some months. Then one of the dwarfs attempted to make contact with her and got an arrow in the arm. He didn't much appreciate that, I suppose. Regardless, the next time Snow White went out, she never returned.

Instead, when the huntsman returned, he ran directly to my chambers, too frightened to pay attention to proper decorum.

"The princess," he whispered to me, his head lowered in shame and urgency lining his grief-wracked voice, "she's gone."

I raised an eyebrow, my lack of emotion perhaps encouraging the rumors that followed, but what could I do? The mirror was watching everything. "What happened?"

He raised his hand, a bloody heart dripping thick, dark fluid down the length of his arm.

"She was playing in a flowering glen when a wild boar approached her. I shot at it with my bow, but some arrows pinged off its back and those that pierced its thick hide made no difference in its speed. I shouted at the princess to run as far and as fast as she could, and I turned my attention to the stampeding beast. It took all my strength and my best hunting knife to slay it. By the time it lay dead, the princess was nowhere to be found. I looked everywhere for her, searched high and low. I brought the boar's heart as proof of my story."

The hunter bowed, waiting for me to release him or order his death. I dismissed him, telling him to wash up and get rid of that disgusting body part.

I tried everything to get the girl back. I disguised myself, brought her lacing strings and tied them so tightly she passed out. I was trying to drag her home when I heard the dwarfs and fled. I tried giving her a comb, laced with a sleeping drug. No, it wasn't poison, as you all like to believe. I could never get her out of the house before the dwarfs' return from the mines.

The mirror, as if sensing my secret activities, began showing me grotesquely detailed bedroom scenes, wherein Snow White whimpered at the hands of the dwarfs.

That's when I smashed the damn thing. I see you looking at my hands. Those scars are full of never-ending, cursed pain. One should never smash a hexed mirror, it turns out.

My time was running out, and I made the apple spell a sleeping enchantment—a sleep so deep that she would appear dead to all. I infected only half of the apple with the charm, leaving the unaffected half white. I would eat some with her in a show of goodwill, as I assumed (and correctly) that she would not take it from me otherwise.

I reasoned the dwarfs would have no use for a lifeless womb and would toss her out. Then I would only have to find her, retrieve her body, and bring her away with me, into hiding or back to her father.

Again, I underestimated them. It is by luck that Queen Snow White is alive today, and luck only.

The morning after I conjured my apple, I snuck over to the cottage, dressed in rags, a spell changing my face to that of an old peddler woman. I called to her, knowing she would not answer. I made as if to trip, and screamed out in fake pain.

The door cracked open just as I was hobbling to my wasted feet.

"Are you all right? Are you very ill?"

I felt a pang of guilt for what I was about to do, but told myself it would all be worth it in the end.

"I'm fine, dear, caring girl. Just old. I've lost my way in these woods, and I've nowhere to sell my wares. I picked these delicious apples just this morning. Would you like to try one?"

She shook her head in timid fashion and the door wavered as she instinctively went to pull it shut. But something stopped her, I'll never know what.

"They said I'm not allowed to open the door to anyone, nor take anything from them. They said all others are meant only to hurt me."

I smiled at her, trying to look as innocuous as possible.

"Surely they couldn't have meant me, child. Look at you! Some fresh fruit would do you much good."

I could see Snow White wanted the apple. It must have been months since she'd last seen fresh fruit. The dwarfs lived solely on meat stews.

"Well," her voice was hesitant, "I'm sure one apple couldn't do any harm."

"That's right." I tried to mask the elation in my voice. "Here, dearie, take my best one." I took the shiny, bewitched fruit from the basket and handed it to her.

"Actually," she balked, "I'd better not. Maybe I'll save it and ask them if I could be allowed a bite this evening."

"Nonsense, love. Look, I'll split it in half. I'll eat it with you. I'd not hurt myself, would I?"

She weighed the offer, then consented.

I ate my half first, proving to her that it caused me no sickness, and she eagerly bit into hers, the juice remaining on her cherry lips as she immediately fell to the ground.

Silently, I edged her foot inside and shut the door. Let the dwarfs think they starved her to death. Let them think they gave her a heart attack. I didn't care about their peace of mind, only that they should not thwart my charms again.

I blew a kiss to her as I left.

The next day, I went to retrieve the princess's body, hoping to revive her in hiding. You can imagine my surprise when I stumbled toward the cottage and saw not a grave, but a glass coffin, Snow White's radiance, even in death, on display for the world to see.

The glass coffin was immovable, unbreakable, impenetrable. I could not budge it. I cried bitter tears, hot streams upon my face as I left her, I thought, for the last time.

But whatever magic was used to seal the coffin kept her pristine. I would sometimes go, during my lonely days, to gaze upon her there, my heart breaking for what I had done.

Years passed. The dwarfs grew older, more feeble. Somehow your young prince managed to convince them to release the coffin into his hands. Perhaps their worship had grown cold on their tongues, for they gave her up to your kingdom.

And for that, I will be eternally grateful.

When news of a royal wedding found its way to my castle, I was overjoyed. I dressed in my most stupendous gown. You do like it, don't you? It matches so well with these burning iron shoes you've placed upon my feet.

I had not expected to be blamed for Snow White's bewitchment, but I accept my fate. If a confession is what you're looking for, I've laid it out for you here, and I tell you in complete honesty that I would do it again a thousand times. I regret nothing.

The pain searing at my feet as you drag me to your madhouse, the flames licking up my calves and legs, they will kill me before long, and I will die happy. For it is I who have saved your precious princess, and her life is worth far more than a deranged old stepmother's ever could be.

Snow

By Donald Weir

Monsieur Rohr arrived at the edge of the map after a few days of bumpy travel. The small kingdom with its small castle surrounded mostly by apple orchards was nothing like the fast paced kingdoms he had left behind.

Monsieur Rohr never understood the purpose of cobblestone. He couldn't remember how many times he had nearly broken an ankle. The clattering of the horse's hooves echoed off the high courtyard walls. He had a headache. His drivers—identical twins—had been prickly ever since their second day at work, when Monsieur Rohr informed them which of the two was handsomer. He'd thought that at least the handsomer of the pair would have been pleased to be told his brother was ugly. Maybe they were causing the horses to be loud on purpose.

The short steward who came to greet him while he was stepping down from his carriage had his nose raised too high, as though he were trying to smell the things a taller man might smell. Monsieur Rohr approved. He, too, only hired very short assistants—it helped everyone remember their place.

"The Monsieur Rohr?" the steward clapped his hands and a flurry of servants dressed in a mismatch of bright colors descended the steps and began unloading the carriages. "Her grace will be most pleased by your visit. She is a huge fan."

"When will dinner be served?" Monsieur Rohr said. He plucked his light blue gloves off his hands. "You may announce my coming to the king."

"Oh, I'm sorry Monsieur. You didn't know?" He said, holding the clipboard behind his back and bowing his head, "The king died, leaving our beloved queen to mourn these past two years."

A dead king. This was perfect.

It was then that Monsieur Rohr saw the little girl scrubbing cobblestones with a hand brush and a bucket of soapy water. She was wearing a brown wool dress and her feet were bare. Her knees were dirty, and a smudge of soot streaked across her cheek. But her clothes and the dirt could not cover up her beauty.

When Monsieur Rohr was a small boy he would go on walks with his mother so that she could teach him about beauty and ugliness. There were eighteen major categories of ugliness, but if you included all the subcategories and miscellaneous factors, he could name more than sixty types of bodily flaws.

He was sure that if his mother hadn't shot herself years ago—the suicide note had one word: wrinkles—then even she would be stunned into silence at the sight of this pure beauty, which had taken the form of a little girl scrubbing stones.

He felt light headed. Her long dark hair framed a face no artist could duplicate. A bard could dedicate his life to creating a song for the vast beauty in her eyes and still die a failure. But it was her complexion that put to shame everything he had once called beautiful.

It was snow. It was the kind of snow that you never forgot. It was the last winter that he spent with his mother as she sat for hours by the window, watching the world's blemishes erase.

"Perfect," he whispered.

The steward led the way up the stairs and Monsieur Rohr followed but every few steps turned to look at her. He wanted to be a part of the song she was humming as she worked.

"Who is that girl?"

The steward turned and took a moment to survey the courtyard. "Ah, you must mean little Snow White. She's the queen's cobblestone cleaner."

"I'm in need of a new assistant."

"I'd be more than happy to suggest some very qualified individuals."

"What if I wanted her?"

The steward took a deep breath like it might be his last. He looked over his shoulder, leaned in and whispered, "I might get my heart cut out and put in a decorative box for telling you this, but the king was not her majesty's first marriage. That little girl is a stepdaughter."

Monsieur Rohr gave him a reassuring nod and then followed him up the steps. Before he entered the castle, though, he couldn't resist taking one last look at little Snow White.

In his prime he could do no wrong. All the princesses and princes in every kingdom watched his every move and imitated him as best they could. If you were powerful, rich, famous, or beautiful, you wore Monsieur Rohr and you paid with gold. But fashion can be fickle, and like a heart that has always pumped without any effort or conscious thought, it too can slow and die without reason. Before Monsieur Rohr's clients melted away, his increasing lack of confidence caused him to more and more frequently make the one decision a fashion designer should never make—no decision. A bad decision can be criticized, but no decision can only be forgotten. As he stared at Snow White, overwhelmed by her beauty, he feared obscurity most of all.

That night there was a feast in his honor. But everyone in the banquet hall was incredibly ugly. The queen herself was at least handsome and seemed pleased to have one of the top designers in all the kingdoms at her court. It was fortunate for Monsieur Rohr—especially for his failed reputation—that news didn't travel fast to this kingdom. In fact, it seemed that not much of anything traveled to this kingdom. Even the more finely tailored clothes looked like they had come out of a wardrobe from twenty years ago—all pointy hats and pastels.

The queen wore a dark purple double cone hat with a black veil draped over it like a mosquito net. She may have been pretty or even gorgeous in her youth. Monsieur Rohr understood she was a dangerous woman. The ugly dukes and duchesses, dressed in unflattering garments, were careful around her.

Monsieur Rohr sat next to the queen. She sat slightly turned in her chair so that she could study him. He knew from years of practice exactly what she was doing. He had scrutinized enough to know when he was being scrutinized.

"Tell me, Monsieur Rohr, what do you think of my court?"

He carefully placed his soup spoon back on the table and gave the room another quick survey. There was an ugly little boy seated between what could only be his parents. All three were gobbling apple pie. He counted seven individuals with foreheads in desperate need of bangs. The lady six seats down from him had the closest set eyes he had ever seen: a Cyclops in a pink dress. The lady sitting next to Cyclops should have been wearing a darker veil. Her nose looked like it belonged to a brawler who had never won a fight. He counted maybe four or five people who didn't have an exhausting list of flaws.

"Pleasant. I feel very welcome here and the food…"

"Monsieur Rohr," she said, rolling the R as though giving it a massage, "Monsieur Rohr, I asked your opinion on my court. I meant your professional, and above all, your honest opinion."

"I'm having a wonderful time here and…"

She leaned in close and looked him dead in the eye. "I want you to tell me if anyone in my court is prettier than me."

She was serious. He could feel his life balancing on this test. Was the gap between the tall man's central and lateral incisors too wide? Did that lady's hair style make her ears look floppy? It was like overanalyzing riding a bike. He felt like he was going to crash.

The queen smiled like she was keeping a secret and began rubbing a piece of her black veil between her fingers.

"The gentleman in the light blue tunic and the thick head of hair is tolerable, your majesty."

The queen ate the rest of her soup without taking her eyes off of the man in the blue tunic. Monsieur Rohr thought that she might call for the man's head on a platter. But she snapped her fingers and a brute peeled away from shadows behind the queen. He leaned down so that she could whisper in his ear. He was hideous, with a huge nose and small dark deep set eyes. A coat of fur covered his forearms and his hands looked like they were made specifically for pounding small animals into heaps of blood and bone. Monsieur Rohr heard her whisper that a walk in the apple orchards would do nicely.

She dismissed the brute with the wave of a hand and turned back to Monsieur Rohr. "I don't believe you met my huntsman."

"No, your majesty," and he hoped that he never would.

The queen gave him very comfortable accommodations in a tower with a huge walk-in closet. He could stay indefinitely, she told him. It wasn't the fast paced lifestyle he had been used to, but between updating the queen's wardrobe, shopping, and sipping pricy wines, he kept busy.

But the reason he didn't run off and find a saner place to retire was a window in his apartment that gave a view of the cobblestone courtyard. He spent his free time watching Snow White. In public he did his best to ignore her, especially in the presence of the queen.

But late at night, when he was alone and the castle was quiet, he made clothes for her. He made extravagant riding dresses with flamboyant matching hats. He made the simplest work clothes, designed to flatter the movements she made while scrubbing. He often worked until the morning sunlight began to tease the night into a soft grey sky. It felt good, like when he was first starting out in the business and he still had hopes to create something worthwhile.

Every few weeks there was another feast. The ugliness that was the queen's court would gather to eat their apple pie and spill grease down their chins and laugh too loud, exposing yellow teeth and receding gum lines.

There were always a couple people at the feast that weren't as ugly as the rest. By the third feast he attended, he was positive that the people he chose each time as fairest were in some unsavory manner, being harmed.

He hinted to the queen that he might like to maybe not make any final decisions or judgments on any one at her court. She calmly reached under the table, grabbed hard at his crotch and gently said, "If I wanted, I could have your testicles nailed to the wall."

He liked his testicles where they were so he remained compliant.

For months he suppressed his emotions. During the day he smiled and laughed and pretended that everything was all right and always would be. And at night he let go of his fears and doubts and guilt and put his soul into making beautiful clothes for Snow White.

In his tower he had always been given the luxury of privacy and peace, so it startled him when he walked in, threw his jacket over the back of an arm chair, and looked up to see the queen. She stood with her back to him at the window overlooking the courtyard. In her hand she clutched a dress. It was his best work, made of a silk that shined like his little Snow White's eyes.

"When I was a little girl I had a dress like this. It was beautiful. It was made just for me".

"Your majesty…"

"Silence," she said like a bone crack. "There will be a feast tonight. You will attend." She left his room, the dress still clutched in her hand.

From the window, Monsieur Rohr watched the queen kick his little Snow White's bucket across the courtyard in a shower of soapy suds. Then she grabbed a fist full of that long perfect hair and used it, like a leash on a frightened puppy, to drag Snow White up the stairs and through the main doors.

He waited at the window, staring at the area she last cleaned, until the water spilled from her bucket had dried up, until the change of guards at the main gate, until the sun went down, and the guests for the feast began to arrive. He feared that he would never see her again.

He dressed in his finest feast day clothes, a blue silk suit, smoothed his hair down, and went to the banquet hall.

They were all there, the queen's court, polluting the air with their disgusting voices and making him want to shield his eyes from their faces. His little Snow White was not there. Maybe she was safe. Maybe the queen had merely sent her away to scrub a different courtyard's cobblestones.

When he sat down next to the queen she gave no hint that anything had happened that afternoon. She complimented the shade of his suit.

After the third course, she leaned over in the customary manner and asked the same question she had asked so many times before.

"Who here, Monsieur Rohr, do you think is prettier than me?"

He surveyed the guests and picked a handsome woman in a bright yellow satin dress, "She is."

"So quick? You barely looked at her," she said. "Have you lost your touch?"

The queen nodded to one of the guards posted at a small side door. He left, and when he returned he was ushering Snow White in front of him.

Only a few noticed her at first but whispers spread throughout the room until there was only silence. The guard nudged her into the center of the room. She was trembling and the dress she wore, his dress, was rumpled. But she was beautiful. It was as though an angel had stumbled into a room full of manure.

Monsieur Rohr realized that he was holding his breath.

"Are you absolutely sure, Monsieur Rohr?" the queen whispered in his ear.

Then he did the only brave thing he had ever done or ever would do in his life. He said yes.

The apple orchards were cold at night. The queen's huntsman shoved them forward when they walked too slowly. The apples that had fallen to the ground looked like rotten hearts in the moonlight. They walked for a long time. Snow White was crying and even the way she cried was pretty, like a little song.

"Run," the huntsman grunted.

At first they stopped and turned to look at him, not sure what to do. He pushed them and they stumbled.

"Run, run, run…" he chanted.

So they ran and for a moment Monsieur Rohr thought that they were free. They were going to make it. He would start a whole new line of clothes and his little Snow White would live a long and happy life.

But it was only a game the huntsman played, giving them a head start. Monsieur Rohr could hear him laughing as he chased after them.

Snow White was too slow and Monsieur Rohr needed to run fast so he did. He didn't mean to leave her behind.

He was running as fast as he could when he heard her beautiful little scream. He looked over his shoulder and before he knocked himself unconscious on a low hanging branch, saw that the brute had her by the neck in one hand. He lifted her high in the air like a doll.

Monsieur Rohr woke to the sound of what he thought were branches breaking. It was still dark and the ground was cold on his cheek. He got to his feet slowly and saw what was really making the noise.

The huntsman was crouched over Snow White's body, snapping ribs out of the way so that there was a gaping hole like a grotesque flower where her chest once was. He was extracting her heart. The huntsman was engrossed in his work. Monsieur Rohr backed away quietly. The last time he saw Snow White's face it looked peaceful, as if she were only sleeping. He ran as far and as fast as he could that night, thankful that his pounding heart was still in his chest.

His near death brought new life to his work. He returned to his old office space and launched a new line just for little princesses—it was a huge success. The little princesses would twirl and giggle and shine.

He regained his reputation as a leading designer and stylist and hired a small army of short assistants.

But sometimes late at night when he was all alone, he would stand at the window of his corner office on the top floor and imagine that his little Snow White was happy and well. He would imagine that she lived in a house in the woods with six or seven of her own short assistants to make sure she was comfortable and had everything she ever needed. She would look up at him and her skin, like falling snow, would break his heart.

Inspired By

Cinderella

Ella

By Katherine Hannula Hill

The room is meant to look homey, cozy even, but doesn't. It's too artificial. I passed two that looked just like it on our way here, down that long hallway, away from the rows of beds and crying children. The woman points to a chair at the table and sits across from me. She's a little too young. A little too well-meaning.

"This is one of our visitation rooms," she says, pointing to the shelf full of children's toys. "We're at full capacity right now and I thought we could hear ourselves think a little better in here." She gives me a small smile and looks down at the papers in front of her. The room encompasses a family home without actually having any of the necessities a family home would, like a kitchen or a bathroom. Instead there's just a bookshelf, a large chair and a large couch. All the surfaces are hard, and glint and flash under the fluorescent lights. The couch and chair aren't covered in cloth but in a cheap waxy fabric designed to make it easy to wipe away a child's unwelcome addition to the room. The woman clears her throat.

"It can be a little overwhelming when you first get here, so let me reintroduce myself." She sticks out her hand. "I'm Helen. Helen Hewitt." I take her hand meekly, trying not to flinch at the pain of lifting my arm. She nervously adjusts her glasses and looks down at the paper in front of her. Bold black font spells ADULT SHELTER CLIENT INTAKE INFORMATION. Next to "NAME OF SHELTER" she writes In Her Shoes.

"I'd prefer not to give my last name and social security number at this time," I say, folding my arms over my chest.

"That's ok. I can understand you're not being ready to share those yet, but we will need them sometime soon, okay?" She brings the paper closer to her body, suddenly aware I'll be able to read what she writes down. "As we talk about why you're here, I'll give you more information about who we are and how we can help you, okay?"

I nod. I watch as she writes Ella next to FIRST NAME. "Ella, that's a pretty name. Is that short for anything?" I'm certainly not going to trust this fidgety woman with my entire first name.

"Yes," I say. I look away from her. "You can skip the whole bit about my address, I'm not telling you that either." She smiles again and nods.

"Let's start out with the more statistical stuff, alright? This won't affect your case at all, it's just data we collect about our clients. Does that make sense?" I nod at the floor. "Ok then. What race do you identify with?"

"White," I say. You'd think my bright blond hair and blue eyes would give that away if the translucence of my skin did not. She circles CAUCASIAN.

"Date of birth?"

"I'll tell you I'm 23."

"Home or cell phone number?" I look her in the eyes. Couldn't they just let me get into bed? I'm exhausted. I'll have to be on the move again tomorrow. I won't be safe until I'm a couple states over.

"I'm not going to tell you any identifying information that could lead him to me, okay? How many times do I have to say it? Just move on to the questions that could apply to any woman." My body hurts and a rage suddenly burns in my throat. "Jesus, any idiot could do your job. Here." I take the papers from her. "Start there." I point to CLIENT'S INCOME. "I don't get any assistance from the state. My husband makes $200,000 per year. I don't have access to that money right now."

I worry he'll use the cards to trace me. He's done it before. I don't even have to be missing 24 hours before the police will search their databases. He's the governor, after all. The well-loved governor. The papers called him "Prince Charming" during the election. That's how I'd met him, actually, at a fundraiser years ago. My wealthy godmother, who had made quite a large contribution to his mayoral campaign that year, insisted I be allowed to go. She even bought me a new dress and new shoes for the occasion. My stepmother fought it, naturally, but she is a powerful woman, my godmother, when she decides she wants something. It didn't seem to bother her that my stepmother "home-schooled" me, which mostly consisted of being locked inside all day and forced to clean and cook for my two stepsisters. She hadn't stepped in then. Of course, my godmother didn't value education. She valued connections and the fundraiser would connect me to the right people, or so I overheard her saying. She had asked about my bruises, but didn't bother with more questions when my stepmother simply said that I was clumsy and often ran into the furniture.

Helen is eyeing me a little more timidly and says with some reservation, "Education?" I look at my options. LESS THAN HIGH SCHOOL. SOME HIGH SCHOOL. HIGH SCHOOL GRADUATE. ATTENDED COLLEGE. COLLEGE GRADUATE. If I were being honest I'd point to LESS THAN HIGH SCHOOL but I hadn't admitted that to anyone and I certainly wasn't going to admit it now.

"Attended college," I say instead.

"Are you employed, Ella?"

"No." A governor's wife was meant to stay at home, in their large house, on their beautifully manicured street.

"Again, this is just for statistical purposes. Did you witness any violence when you were growing up?" I pause. I wouldn't say I witnessed a lot of violence, but I certainly experienced it. "Anything between your mom and dad you'd like to share with me at this time?" I shake my head and then worry that's not final enough.

"No."

"Who referred you to our shelter, Ella?"

"My doctor." He had done his best to ignore it. He's a friend of the family, naturally, and had been my husband's doctor when he was a child. But after four years even he couldn't convince himself I was that clumsy.

"Did you come directly from your home, Ella?" I nod and watch her circle HOME WITH ABUSER under HOUSING.

"You're married to the person who caused you those injuries, Ella?" I nod again. "Have you filed for a divorce?" I look her directly in the eyes.

"He'd kill me."

"Okay. Thank you for sharing that. I'm just trying to get an idea of your legal situation." ABUSER RELATIONSHIP: SPOUSE.

"How long have you two been married?"

"Three years."

"How long did you know him before you married?"

"Two years." I was just 18 when we met. My stepmother had assured me I had not completed the necessary requirements to graduate and that I'd need to stay home another year. Another year of cooking and cleaning and clumsiness.

In the home where first my mother, bringing me into this world, died and then my father. My stepmother had done everything to help my father as he succumbed slowly to a heart attack. She'd called 911. She'd yelled and begged and cried. That is the one nice thing I can say about my stepmother. She loved my father.

My stepmother wanted Prince Charming around, but not with me. She'd send me on a task in the kitchen and summon her daughters to keep him company. I stopped inviting him to the house, and after six months of fighting to see me and sneaking around, he got sick of it.

He bought me a condo and I moved in the minute he signed the papers. My own walls. My own rules. Or so I thought. It didn't take him long to point out that he would rather have the sofa facing towards the window and dinner ready by the time he got there. I didn't think much of it at the time. Those seemed like minor adjustments after my stepmother. In the condo there was criticism but never brutality. Never black eyes. Never bruises. He saved that for our marriage. Only a few weeks after we said "I do" he was elected governor. I kept telling myself the stress changed him.

He really was prince charming when we first met. I'd felt nervous in my expensive dress that night. My godmother had insisted I get my hair and nails done and I was nervous a sudden movement would ruin the whole thing, so I stood as still as possible. Until he'd asked me to dance. He was handsome in his tux. His hair slicked back and his eyes bright and blue. Eyes that made you feel like you were the only girl in the room. Or at least that's how I'd felt. As we danced he made me smile and feel at ease for the first time. He asked me questions about what I liked in a way that no one really had before.

I felt like such a fool when my heel broke. I'd never danced in heels before and I must have stepped on it wrong. He'd caught me as I fell in his big, strong arms. He helped me over to a chair and quickly had someone fetch some glue. When he went to talk to a couple of his biggest supporters and answer a few quick questions from the reporter, he made me promise not to move from that spot until he got back. One of the interns working for him helped me glue the heel back on and I sat in that exact spot as promised.

Photographers' flashes followed him as he walked over to me. Taking it gently from my hand, he got down on one knee and slipped the shoe back on my foot. He smiled up at me before standing and, taking me by the hand, walked me back to the dancefloor. At 18 you think things like my heart has wings. I felt I could touch every star in the sky if he was with me. Two hours later he looked me in the eyes and said, "It took 36 years but now I know." I blushed and asked him what he meant. "So, this is love." This was the miracle that I'd been waiting for. I knew then I would no longer have to be afraid of my stepmother. He would save me.

"Have the police ever been called?" I shake my head.

"It's okay if you don't want to answer this question," she looks up from her papers apologetically. "Were you ever raped by your abuser?" I'm not sure for a moment what to say. I'm not sure I can make her see. I used to think I could show people. The first night he'd hurt me I'd run. I'd taken a cab as far as my fifteen dollars would get me and then I'd walked to the beautiful home of the woman who had once saved me. She could save me again. My godmother took one look at me and sent me straight to the bathroom. After a hot shower, a blow dryer, and a pair of her pajamas, I sat down with her. The coffee she gave me burned hot in my shaking hands.

She looked me over calmly and asked, "Have you been drinking, Cinderella?" My hand raised to my mouth. I had been drinking. "There's nothing to be embarrassed about, as long as we don't embarrass ourselves." She smoothed a wrinkle in her shirt. "You chose to marry him. You chose to be a public figure." I tried to interject, nearly spilling my coffee. She holds up her hand and I lose the words. "Everyone has fights." She cleared her throat. "Everyone has one too many." She looked me in my bloodshot eyes. "I wish I could say a quick bippity boppity boo and fix all of this, but it's not that simple. All we can do is do better next time." She took the coffee from my hand and set it down on the table. "I'm going to let you two sort this out." She left the room, the walls spinning as I tried to understand what she was saying. "He explained the whole thing." She brought him into the room. There was his handsome face and shining hair and his hands. Large hands that just a few hours ago had hurt me, had humiliated me -- she was asking him to sit down.

"Ella," he said, reaching to put his hand on my leg. I flinched and turn away, causing my head to pound and the tears to fall.

"He's going to take you home now, dear. He understands you have a problem with alcohol and he and I are going to get you help." My godmother smiled at me. "Why don't you come with me and you can pick out a warm coat." I followed her obediently to the closet and through the fog in my head I tried to tell her what had happened. She grabbed at one of the coats and said cheerfully, "This one will be lovely on you." In a last attempt to make her see I pulled the pajama top down over my shoulder, exposing the large hand-shaped bruises on my upper arm. "We're going to get you help, Ella. You were out of control. He told me how you were hysterical, throwing yourself at the wall and hitting your head. He grabbed you to make you stop." She gently pulled the pajama sleeve up over my shoulder. "Tonight you need rest in your own bed with your husband. Tomorrow you start thinking about what to do to get the help you need." She led me back to him. My godmother and my prince charming exchanged concerned looks over my head and I followed him, defeated, to the car. This woman had asked if he'd raped me? If my own godmother couldn't see, how would this woman? After 'I do' I stopped making choices, but here, now, I can choose not to answer.

"Do you have children who have seen the abuse?"

"No."

"Were you ever pregnant?" She takes my arms falling quickly to my flat stomach as a yes. "Was there abuse during the pregnancy?" I swallow and nod. She is the first person I've ever told that to. She hands me the Kleenex box. She has the decency to wait a couple of minutes while

I collect myself, but I notice she is checking the clock. It's 6:15. She probably wants to get home.

"Are you alright to continue?" I nod. She smiles and looks down at the next question. "Any chemical dependencies we should be aware of?" I can't begin to think about any of that right now and I shake my head. "It's very common for women in your situation to turn to drugs or alcohol, no one is blaming you--"

"No." I have to stop myself from shouting it. Something in my tone makes her move on to the next page. She hesitates, looking over the set of questions carefully. "Let me look at those." I turn the page towards me. "You can circle all of them." Under the heading ABUSE TYPES BY ABUSER, she loops black ovals around the words: STALKING. CONFINEMENT. PHYSICAL. VERBAL/EMOTIONAL/PSYCHOLOGICAL. DESTRUCTION OF PROPERTY/PETS. RAPE/SEXUAL. WEAPONS THREATENED OR USED. I wish I had not seen the word pets. Poor Jack and Gus. My husband hadn't thought mice were appropriate pets for the mayor's wife. One day as we were arguing -- something trivial about not buying the right detergent -- he'd let them out of their cage. I'd found them a couple days later in a large mouse trap. Poor Gus had tried to chew off his paw but he'd bled to death before he could get away.

"Knife. Hands. Feet." I point to the next question, WEAPONS USED. She circles them, leaving GUN, FIRE, NONE and OTHER. She leans back, lifting the paper slightly so I can't read it.

"I'm going to ask you some questions about your abuser--" she puts her hands up defensively before I've gotten a chance to say anything. "I know you don't want to share any identifying information, so I'll skip down to the more general questions." I'm not going to thank her, so I just nod.

"Race?"

"White."

"Height?" I consider this. A lot of men are tall.

"Six feet. Two inches."

"Weight?" A lot of men are fit.

"180."

"Hair?" Shiny. Sleek. Perfectly in place.

"Black."

"Eyes." Bewitching. Quick to change.

"Blue."

"Education?"

"Law school."

"Work status?"

"I'm not going to tell you what he does."

"You said before he was employed. That's all I'm asking here."

"Yes, he's employed."

"Did he witness any violence as a child?"

"I don't know." It had never come up. He certainly held up his mother as the perfect housewife. An expectation I had not lived up to. He didn't talk much about his father.

"Does he have any identifying marks? I know you don't want us to know who he is, but if he came here tonight it would help us to recognize him. If we can recognize him we can keep you safe." If he comes here tonight, no one is going to be able to keep me safe. Identifying marks. I think about the question for a minute. He didn't have any distinguishing or identifying marks, it was part of what made him prince charming. Dark-haired, blue-eyed, classically handsome prince charming.

"Does he have access to a gun?"

"Yes."

"I can't imagine how hard this is for you." She sighs and I think she is tempted to put her hand on my arm so I pull it off the table. "We are almost done, but can I get you something to drink before we go on?" I want this to be over. I want to lay down. I shake my head. She nods, as if to say she knew I would say that. She flips to the next page and lays it down in front of me. There is a sterile drawing of a naked woman. She has no nipples or facial features. Next to her are the words ABRASION. BRUISE. BROKEN BONE. PUNCTURE WOUND. OTHER. "Can you point to a couple of places where you have current injuries?" I point to the naked woman's neck, her right wrist, her stomach, and her left thigh.

"Do you need me to show you?" I choke a little on the words and close my eyes.

"No," she says. "That's not necessary right now unless you think you need medical attention." I shake my head.

"They're mostly just bruises this time." She gives me a pitying look and then stands up.

"Thank you so much for taking the time to answer all of those questions. I know that's not easy." She walks towards the door, but doesn't urge me to follow. "If you'll just wait here a minute, I'll see if we can get you into a room."

I feel a weight lift off my shoulders the moment I'm alone. I move to the couch, worried I'll fall to the floor of exhaustion if I spend even one more minute on that hard chair. I'm tempted to lay down. Every other time I've left and answered these questions, I've laid down, closed my eyes and convinced myself I just need one night to be in a safe place. Tomorrow would be different. I've told myself I'll go back to the house just to grab a few things. If he's there, he'd be different. He'd be more like the man I first met. The man that so gently slid the shoe back on my foot and danced with me till midnight. The man who rescued me from my evil stepmother and made me believe love at first sight was real.

I force myself back to the chair, taking in every ache in my body as I straighten my back against its cold one. I can see him now, hear him as he tells me "So, this is love." I kept coming back to those words, fighting for them and suddenly I see. So, this is him. Abuser. Perpetrator. Those were the words the well-meaning girl had used for him. I stand up, nearly bumping into the woman as she opens the door. She looks sad and desperate for a moment, as if she is used to women leaving.

"Please. Let's talk more about what we can do--"

"Can you get me hair dye?" She looks confused for a moment and then nods.

"I am pretty sure another client left some here last week. If not I'll get you some." I take in her dark auburn hair and light eyebrows for the first time.

"I've never done it before…" I raise my eyes from my feet to her face. "Would you help me?" She smiles and nods.

Five AM the next morning, I step out in my red hair and lost-and-found black hoodie. By the time he traces the ATM charge I'll be on a train. She had asked me where I wanted to go. The ocean was all I could think to say. When he wakes up 55 minutes later, the train will be pulling out of the station. When he is finished with his morning push-ups, hot shower, and eggs I'll be crossing the state line.

I settle into the soft seat, feeling the wheels rumble below me. Prince Abusive. Perpetrator Charming. This was the miracle that I've been dreaming of. I'd finally dropped his mask. By the time it falls back in place, I'll be gone.

Fairy Godmother

By David W. Landrum

I told no one of the circumstances by which I became Queen. People would have thought me mad if I had given them the details. And I had to be careful. Treachery at the palace is intense. I quickly discovered how the wealthiest families in our kingdom plotted incessantly against the royals, maneuvering to seize power and increase their land holdings. You have to use wisdom in dealing with them. My humble beginnings worked to my advantage in this case. The men and women from the most powerful and most treacherous clans knew I had been a slave in my old home and assumed my old status meant I was illiterate and naïve.

They attempted to destroy me by telling me ludicrous stories: the Prince had only married me because he wanted to eat my children when they were born; he turned into a hideous beast at night; he would impregnate me with demon children; he was a worshipper of the Devil and would soon insist I participate in obscene rites involving perversion and human sacrifice. I acted frightened, let them propose I poison him, and then I would clap my hands and the faithful servants and ministers of our courts would come out of their hiding places and arrest the plotters. Two were hanged. Five estates paid heavy fines for their attempts to deceive me; titles of nobility were stripped from their families. They were angry but also afraid. I won't say they stopped plotting against me, but they knew they would have to adopt new tactics. This gave me a little breathing room—breathing room to pursue my main ambition.

Of course, a Queen must give birth to heirs, and I did this quiet well. Oslac and I had four children in the next three years—three sons and a daughter. All of them were strong and healthy. The kingdom had heirs. I told the midwife I wanted no more children. She gave me herbs she said would end my childbearing. I took them, sickened, and thought she had poisoned me, but I recovered. My blood still came monthly, but I did not get pregnant again after that.

During the years of my childbearing I hired tutors who instructed me in history and religion, I had taught myself to read when I was living with Tremaine, my stepmother, and my stepsisters Druzella and Anastasia, but I had trouble getting books and finding time to read. My tutors opened my mind to many marvelous things. When your mind is open and when you have leisure to think, wonder and contemplate, your curiosity will settle on the things you want to know above all else.

I called the midwife, Élodie, whom I knew I could trust, and asked the question that had begun to burn in my heart.

"Who was my fairy godmother, Élodie?"

"I don't know, Queen Elaine." She paused and then added, "But I think I might be able to find out."

"I will reward you if you do."

She only nodded. A week later she returned.

"Please you, my Queen. I did not find out a great deal, but I did find out her name. It is Alura. She dwells in our kingdom, though I was not able to discover where. I'm sorry this is all the information I could gather."

I gave her gold and told the Grand Duke to grant her family additional land to farm. For the next few days I brooded over the thin wisp of knowledge I had accrued. One morning just after Oslac and I made love, the solution dawned on me. I knew her name. There was someone in the Kingdom who could tell me where she might be found. I contacted Élodie again.

"His house is in the wood of Deverell," she said. "It is a danger to go there, though. If your enemies find out, they will accuse you of sorcery; many of their relatives hold high positions in the Church. I would not advise going to see him. And how could you get there without someone knowing?"

That was a difficulty. I set my mind to solving the problem and came up with a solution a week later. I announced that I planned to make a pilgrimage to the shrine of Saint Gertrude of Nivelles, which lay at the edge of Deverell Wood.

That would involve riding. I remembered riding as a child with my father—before Mother died, Father remarried, and then Father died and Tremaine made me a servant so my riding lessons ended. At the palace I had begun to learn to again. I made quick progress. The rhythms of it were in my body's memory, and the skill I had learned and loved surfaced after so many years once I felt motion of a horse under my legs again. After two months of diligent practice, I had some mastery of riding and made plans to set out.

Oslac had just left on a diplomatic trip to Gascoigne, which is why he had made sure to thoroughly fuck me every morning and night for a week. I could trust Grand Duke Bertrand to manage things while I was absent. No one would question my desire to venerate an honored saint. I could slip off in the night and visit Burnell, who was rumored to be a sorcerer.

I travelled with an entourage, as a Queen must—soldiers, servants, grooms, officials who went before us and made arrangements for food and lodging. I might have asked a nun or two to accompany me as spiritual advisers, but the ruling families often sent daughters to local convents and I did not know of a nun I could trust. I said I felt a little queasy, thought I might be pregnant, and wanted Élodie, the midwife, to accompany me.

We rode four days. I worshipped at the shrine, asking the Saint to help me find the truth. I feigned sickness that night and said I would feel safer if Élodie slept with me rather than one of my maidens, a queen is seldom alone—someone always sleeps with me, either in my bed or somewhere in the room; I hardly know privacy and solitude. At midnight, we slipped out through a window and went to the stables to get the horses ready for our ride to Burnell's home. I knew how to saddle a horse from days as a slave to Tremaine, but when Élodie and I sneaked into the stalls, someone stood in the door, lantern in hand, blocking our entrance.

"You don't need to be afraid, Queen Elaine. I thought I would spare you the ride to my house in the wood. Saint Gertrude apparently heard your prayer and interceded for you."

I was so scared I thought I might wet myself and had to squeeze my secrets parts together to prevent it. When I recovered, I spoke.

"I'm sorry. You startled us. You are Burnell, I take it."

"And ever your servant."

"You knew my prayer to the saint; I assume you also know why I've come here."

"Your arrival is fortuitous. Alura is under an enchantment and must be freed from it."

"How is she under an enchantment? Isn't she a magic being with great power?"

"She is, but magical beings have enemies. Evil fairies cast spells to harm benevolent fairies who are powerful but not careful. Alura is under an enthrallment cast by an ancient, evil sorcerer. Only one of her own blood can free her."

"Where can I find such a creature—a creature of her blood? Tell me, and tell me where Alura dwells and I'll bring whoever it is to her side."

"Where can you find such a 'creature'?" He laughed at the term I had used. "Simple. Look in the mirror."

"What do you mean?" I stammered.

"You are her child. She is your mother, not your fairy godmother."

Shock went through me. I gaped, unable to speak. I felt wobbly and very un-Queen-like.

"How can this be?" I demanded.

"Do you remember your mother?"

"Barcly. I was only five years old when she died."

"Did you see her die?"

"I did not."

"Did you go to her funeral? Do you even know where she's buried?"

"My stepmother kept all of this from me."

"She kept all of it from you because your mother, Alura, did not die. She is under an enchantment and you are the one who must free her. Listen to me. I can't much longer sustain the spell that makes your attendants oblivious to what is going on. You need to go to her."

"Go to her and do what? Where is she? Where does she dwell? How can I free her?"

He smiled. "All things are revealed to her who seeks. You've found that out already. I must go now. Return to your chamber. No one will see you and Élodie. Go back to bed. As proof that the words I speak are true, I tell you the future. Jocelyn, one of your trusted servants, will try to kill you at breakfast in the morning. She will have a dagger concealed in her garments. Have guards posted to seize her when she makes the attempt. Capture her alive so you may question her. Return now."

And he was gone.

Élodie and I stood there, too stunned to move.

"We'd better get out of here," I finally said.

We returned to my bedchamber, not climbing back through the window but walking through the front door of the inn. The guards, a few revelers who were still drinking, and the whores doing their business did not notice us. We went to the room, undressed, and climbed in bed. We were frightened, to say the least. I could hardly believe Jocelyn would attempt to murder me, but I also knew Burnell's power of second sight. Élodie finally dropped off to sleep. I heard the watchman call out two a.m. and finally slept myself. In the morning, no one made mention of the two of us being gone.

Questions swarmed in my mind like sparrows in an abandoned barn. I wondered what Burnell meant and why he did not specifically tell me where Alura was and how I could free her from the spell. Sorcerers always speak in riddles. And Alura was my mother. My mind spun around so much I had to sit and calm myself. Of course, Burnell had not been cryptic about what Jocelyn meant to do, and this gave me focus so the astonishment I felt did not immobilize me. I ordered breakfast, concealed two guards behind the tapestries near my bed, and told Élodie to busy herself packing my trunks. Jocelyn brought in my tray. I reflected as I watched her bring it to me with a smile on her face and a greeting in God's name how the human heart is so twisted and capable of deceit. She knew I liked to eat with only one or two servants in attendance. She had won my trust with faithful service and now meant to murder me. She set the tray of bacon and porridge on the table behind which I sat. When I looked down at it, she drew a dagger from between her breasts and raised it to stab me.

I dropped to the floor. She swung the blade and missed. By that time the soldiers had bolted out of hiding. They seized and disarmed her. I stood. The rest of my entourage rushed into the room. Expressions of astonishment and disgust covered the faces of everyone. The guards held Jocelyn, who looked mad with terror. I took the knife with which she had meant to kill me from one of the guards.

"Jocelyn, you have torn my heart by your treachery. This is not a time for many words, so give me up the truth. If you don't answer me, we'll see if the rack can loosen your tongue—or the scavenger's daughter or the pear of anguish."

I smelled urine and saw a pool of it form at her feet. She stared, unable to speak. I nodded to the guards to take her away.

"No, my Queen. Have mercy. Please don't put me on the rack. I'll tell you everything."

"Who suborned you?"

She looked about uneasily. I understood. I told the guards to bind her securely and then ordered everyone to leave the room. They obeyed reluctantly. Jocelyn couldn't move and I had the knife. When we were alone, I leveled my gaze at her. Her lips trembled.

"You will die soon. Don't go before the Judgment Seat of Christ with the sin of concealing treason on your heart. Who suborned you?"

"The Grand Duke, Bertrand."

I tried not to react. Immediately, though, surges of fear shot through my body, hot as lightning. If the Grand Duke had tried to murder me and was taking advantage of Oslac's absence to seize power, he would have taken over the palace. My children were there.

"Do you have proof of this?" I asked. It was difficult to talk because my mouth had gone dry.

"There is a letter. It is concealed in my bodice, beneath my left breast."

I called Élodie in and had her retrieve the letter. I read, unable to believe what it said. The Grand Duke had seized power. He told Jocelyn that he had sent assassins to slay Oslac and that she would be greatly rewarded when she killed me. By the time I was dead, he assured her, he would have seized the palace and 'sequestered', this was the word he used, the royal family. After reading this, I called my guard and a trusted Council member back in.

"Fetch a priest," I ordered, "so this young woman may confess and be absolved. When that is done, hang her from the tree in the front of the inn. Look to it."

They nodded and carried the sobbing, pleading maiden out of my bedchamber. I think she had imagined I would spare her for telling me the truth. I gave Randolph, the Councilor, the letter and told him to share it with the other officials I had brought along and with the Captain of my personal guard. I told them I wanted to be alone for a few moments. They left the room, posting a guard at the door.

When she was gone, I sat down and wept. My children. What did he meant by 'sequestered'? Did he simply mean to imprison them, or were they dead already? Had he had them strangled or suffocated? I had put such thoughts out of my mind or I would go mad. I needed to be decisive. If a chance of saving them existed, it would hang on my response to his seizure of power. To think that one of my most trusted women, a woman who had served me at table, slept with me to keep me warm on winter nights, bathed and dressed me, had tried to murder me was almost more than I could bear. And the Grand Duke, whom I had trusted, had proved a traitor. Even now I was in danger of his sending soldiers to kill me. I had to move quickly, though I was not even certain what I would do. I ordered the groom to saddle our horses. We would leave our baggage at the inn. Speed was essential.

When the groom said our steeds were ready, we hurried down the stairs and out of the inn for the stables. A crowd had gathered in front of the inn. The troops assigned to the hanging were tying Jocelyn's hands behind her back and getting the rope ready. We went to the stables and mounted up. By the time we rode out the guards has hoisted her and she was kicking and flailing, eyes, bulging, mouth open, tongue hanging out. I rode past her. We would head for the garrison at Skeleton Path. We rode past Deverell Wood and on toward the mountains. I dispatched riders to other garrisons and to our border fortresses and bases. I needed an army and hoped our troops at locations outside the capitol would be loyal. I sent riders to catch up to Oslac, warn him, and tell him what had happened. I also sent scouts ahead to the villages that lay en route to Skeleton Path. I needed to know if they were still loyal to Oslac and me. I tried not to worry about my children, but this was impossible.

We passed through Willow Grove, more of a small town than a village. The people flocked to greet us. They knelt, cheered, and shouted 'Long live King Oslac, Long live Queen Elaine'. The leading men of the town told me what they had so far learned.

Messengers had arrived that very morning informing them that I had been murdered by a servant girl. Because the King was far away, the Grand Duke said he had taken control of the palace and made himself temporary ruler of the land. I read a copy of the proclamation Bertrand had sent out. He assured everyone he would relinquish control of the kingdom upon Oslac's return. In the letter he said he had secured the royal children in the fortress of Whitby Bluff. That was half a day's journey from here. Of course, he might have sent them there so they could be murdered at a more remote location. As I thought on it more, I found a slip of hope in the fact that Oslac and I were popular. The people venerated us. My husband was not a harsh ruler and the kingdom had prospered under his rule. The Grand Duke would have to be careful. He could not blatantly seized power. He meant to have my husband killed and probably would say the King of Gascoigne was responsible, just as he would have blamed Jocelyn for my death. With both of us out of the way, he could then move against our children, but I doubted he would harm them before he had completely secured power in our land.

I assembled the fighting men of the village. Our standing army is small, standing armies are expensive to maintain, but our militia numbers in the thousands and can be called up on short notice. The mayor called a muster, and men who had fought and who had weapons rallied to me. Willow Grove supplied forty soldiers with arms and horses. I had assembled a force. Hopefully, as word got out, the people of Willow Grove hastened to spread the word to nearby settlements, I could build up a sizeable force quickly.

Late morning, we set out for Skeleton Path. The Fortress got its name for the road that leads to it, a natural basalt path some twenty feet wide shot through with long, thin veins of white stone that truly look like human bones and, in some places, resemble full skeletons. Many legends purport to explain the origins of the stones patterns, none of which I imagined were true. As we rode, a group of riders approached. My troops formed around us, but the riders approached with assurances of good will and bowed the knee when they caught sight of me.

We conferred. They had been told of my demise. Word had come from Whitby's Bluff that the children of the royal family had been sent there for safety and were well.

A weight lifted off my soul. My children were alive—still in dire circumstances and vulnerable, but alive.

"Why would the commander of Whitby be so eager to inform you of this?" I asked Raeldwald, the Commandant of the Garrison at Skeleton Path.

He simply said, "My brother."

I thanked God—though the thanks might be more properly directed to Burnell's magic or my mother's. I pondered, knowing I needed to be quick and decisive.

"Mobilize your garrison," I told the Commandant. I don't know how I remember this; I suppose I had heard my husband, speak of it once. "Your unit consists of fifty, does it not?"

"Yes, my lady." He was surprised I knew. With his men added to my cohort that would give me a force of over eighty.

"We ride to Whitby. Is your brother loyal to us?"

"He is your captain, my Queen. The Grand Duke sent his brother, Guthrun, and a force of twelve guards there. My brother suspected treachery from the beginning. He doesn't like Guthrun and resents his proclaiming himself provisional ruler of the fort."

The Whitby Fortress was larger than Skeleton Path. It was, in fact, our largest garrison, housing one hundred men, and it guarded a strategic pass that had often been a corridor for invaders bent on conquering our land. A garrison city abutted the fortress.

"Did your brother say where my children are being lodged?" I asked after we had ridden a long way in silence.

"No, my Queen."

But I had a good notion where they might be. We stopped for the night in a small village, which generously fed us and added three fighting men to our number. In the morning we rode until we moved into the town that had grown up around the fortress. As I had suspected, they had put my daughter and my two youngest boys in care of nuns at Saint Bertha of Kent. I went and rejoiced to see them safe. They wept, saying the Grand Duke had told them I had been murdered. I simply told them he was mistaken. They looked in good health, and while I rejoiced to see them safe, my joy had to be qualified. My eldest son, Audric, the heir apparent to the throne, was in the castle with the Grand Duke's son, Guthrun.

I went into the chapel and knelt before the altar. I did not pray. After a moment, I settled on a plan, rose, and went out. My troops assembled. We rode to the fortress. By now they had heard we were nearby. Guthrun had ordered the fortress closed up.

When we approached the fort, he appeared on the battlements. My son stood by his side. Two guards held him. I assumed they were Guthrun's men and not regulars from the garrison.

I knew I needed to speak first.

"Guthrun," I called out. "Surrender. Your cause it lost."

"That remains to be settled, Cinder-Queen. I have your son. Shall I toss you his head?"

"Harm one hair of his head and I will erase the house of Colville from the face of the earth and have you flayed alive. You see my troops. Even if you manage to have Oslac murdered, they will follow me. The countryside is rallying to my standard. Surrender and there may be mercy for you." A course of action occurred to me then. I had to act on it without second-guessing my instincts. I dismounted and walked forward. Raeldwal and two of his officers climbed off their mounts and scampered toward me.

"Queen Elaine, don't present yourself unguarded to this entourage of traitors," Raeldwal pleaded.

I turned to face him. "You don't need to fear for me, Raeldwal. Eternal good shields me, let treason do what it will. Step back. Respect my wish."

He hesitated but stepped back. I walked forward.

What I did seems foolish now. I presented myself as a target to Guthrun's scoundrels. One of them could have easily killed me with a bolt or an arrow. Divinity, it is said, hedges a monarch. I only hoped the proverb would hold true. I stopped about ten feet from the gate and looked up.

"Men of Whitby Fortress," I said. "You have been deceived by this foul traitor." Guthrun gaped. He assumed I had walked forward to negotiate with him. "I do not ask you to throw down your weapons." I pointed, raising my voice. "I order you to instead free my son, your Prince, and throw down this pretender to the throne."

What happened next happened in mere seconds. The two men guarding my son jolted from the deadly force of several bolts punching into their bodies. Someone seized Audric. This filled me with terror until I recognized Faron, Raeldwal's brother, as the one who had taken my son away from the wall.

A moment later, the soldiers obeyed my commandment literally. They hurled Guthrun down from the battlements. Screaming, he fell twelve feet, hitting the pavement with a sickening thump only a few feet away from me. His blood splattered the front of my dress. A second later, the gates opened. Faron came out with my son, who broke from him and ran to me.

Decorum be damned, I thought. Queen, yes, but I am a mother and a woman. The vague thoughts I had of appearing stern and unmoved dissolved when Audric ran up to me, arms out, crying, "Mother!" I enfolded him in my arms and wept. The soldiers of Whitby emerged and knelt to show their loyalty. I wanted to acknowledge their loyalty but I couldn't stop crying. I squeezed my five-year old son's warm body—his living body—and wept. After a while, though, I knew I had to resume my role as Queen and sovereign. I gave Auturic to Raeldwal.

"Men of Whitby," I said. "Your loyalty will not be forgotten. Are the traitors who accompany this man secured?"

Faron said they were.

"Bring them out and take their heads this very moment."

He obeyed. Two of Gudrun's troupe had been killed already. The loyal soldiers brought the ones still alive and decapitated them in my presence. I fought with all my strength not to vomit or swoon at the sight of it, I had sent Auturic back to the convent. I ordered the heads of all the traitorous men sent to the place and to the Grand Duke.

Guthrun was still alive. I ordered my troops flay him. He was not hurt so badly that he would not feel it. I would send his head and his hide to the Capitol.

My actions later earned me the epithet, "the Bloody Virgin," which made me laugh because by the time I order those killings I had been fucked from one end of my bedchamber to the other and had given birth to four children. Still, it stuck and became a by-word. Others called me Queen Elaine the Just because I had ordered the executions in response to the crime of treason. That caught on as well, and I became known by both titles through the years. Paradoxes come at us in this manner. It's something that keeps life amusing.

By the time Oslac returned I had rallied the kingdom and surrounded the castle. The Grand Duke had sent assassins to kill my husband. They attacked him at a banquet and wounded him. Oslac offered them a merciful death if they named who had hired them. They said it was Bertrand and produced a letter from him admitting them to the king's table at the banquet. My beloved received a stab wound in the shoulder, deep but not life-threatening, and a cut across the face that left a horrible scar. It made me love him even more—in fact, once he became not so "perfect," my love for him increased. It was the experience of treason and danger that truly bonded us. After this, we governed our kingdom as co-rulers.

We executed Bertrand, confiscated his land, and punished those who were his confederates with fines, exile, and, in some cases, death. The kingdom settled down to stability once again. Our land prospered.

But for me, there remained the matter of my mother.

I tried to contact Burnell, but no one could find him. "If he doesn't wish to be found, he will not be found," Élodie told me. And I could not or discover anything else concerning where my mother, sleeping, ensorcelled, might be found.

Months passed. Winter came. I had just come from frolicking with my children in the snow and we were warming ourselves in front of the fireplace in the throne room when the Lord Chamberlain and two other officials entered and asked audience. They said the matter they wished to present needed urgent attention. I sent the children away with our serving women and went through the formalities an official audience required: my girls brought me my robe and crown, which I hated to wear; the robe was hot, the crown gave me a kink in my neck when I wore it for any length of time; I hoped the matter they wanted me to judge would be brief. I sat on the throne. A serving maiden brought my scepter. Two guards and two ladies-in-waiting flanked me. I was all set up now.

The Chamberlain explained. A woman in Wedmore had been convicted of sorcery. She had appealed the conviction and petitioned for me to judge her appeal. Since my ascension as Queen, we had passed a law that any woman sentence to death could appeal to me. In the years of my reign I had judged eight cases under this law. Four I had pardoned; four had been clearly guilty and received no reprieve.

The woman worshipped Freya, and it was this that made it a sensitive issue. Oslac's grandfather had allowed worship of the old gods in Wedmore, a province where the ancient practices and beliefs had hung on. Pagan temples abounded there. In fact, the pagans in the province outnumbered the Christians just slightly. Church officials had arrested the girl for practicing magic, which is against the law throughout our land. She claimed she performed the magic as a part of her worship of the goddess, a thing permitted under the decree of fifty years ago. The officials pointed out that her conjurations did not take place in the Temple of Freya and were in no way related to the worship rites offered the goddess for centuries, thus falling under the definition of sorcery. They had sentenced her to be burned. The province guarded our northern border. Powerful enemies lay on the other side of our boundaries and they were more than willing to make trouble for us.

When I talked it over with Oslac he said it might be a good idea to judge the case and to judge it immediately.

The pagans in Wedmore were restive because of what had happened. Tension between them and the Christians there had been growing over the last few years and some nasty incidents had exacerbated ill feelings. The countries that bordered Wedland encouraged the strife because they wanted to annex the province. If they were able to do so, it would be almost impossible to guard our northern states.

I assembled the Council and agreed to judge the case. The officials smiled, relieved.

"Is the girl imprisoned?" I asked.

They said that she was.

"Release her after she has sworn an oath in the name of the goddess Freya that she will meet with me to discuss the appeal."

"My Queen," the Chamberlain said, suddenly dismayed, "she will flee."

"If she does, it will disgrace the name of the goddess, discredit the girl, and strengthen the testimony of the church in that province. See that she is release at once—provided she will swear the oath."

They left. I made preparations. Travel is difficult and dangerous in winter. Wedmore lay a week's journey away. I decided I would make it a progress—I would slowly move from village to village and town to town, staying in the houses of local officials, greeting our subjects, and honoring their loyalty.

In my years as Queen, I had won the affection of our people. I did not try to do this in any particular way, but it somehow happened. The people loved me, perhaps because I was not raised in a way that isolated me from the common folk. My family was in the lower-ranking nobility, but after Father died I found myself largely among the commoners. I milked cows, worked in the yard, cook and cleaned, and as I did I met every day folk. I bought food in the local market, helped slaughter pigs and cattle, assisted people planting vegetables and harvesting. Through those years I learned the goodness, sincerity, and wisdom of the common people. I learned their speech, which is sometimes more like a foreign language than a dialect. I don't want to foolishly idealize commoners. They cheated me out of money at times, taunted and mocked me, calling me 'Cinder-Ella', because I was often dirty from cleaning the hearth; once a man tried to drag me into a cowshed and molest me. Still, what I encountered most often was a plain, winsome goodness. People loved me because I understood them and treated them with dignity. Oslac told me our subjects' love for me secured the kingdom more firmly than an army of a hundred-thousand. Making a progress would be a good strategy to further cement our peoples' loyalty and would be an easier, safer way to journey in winter than trying to travel straight through in the snow and bad weather.

The progress proved a success. People flocked to see me, braving the cold. I blessed babies and new brides, met with thousands of my subjects, tasted wonderful food and wine, I had to be careful not to eat too much, occasionally slept in peasant homes and dined with the lowly; I worshiped in simple churches; I listened to rustic music and saw performances of old morality plays, farces, and dramas. At length I arrived in Wedmore. After a few days visiting and doing all I had done in other locations the past two months, I came to judge the case of the girl, whose name was Sheena.

Snow fell the day of the hearing. The officials told me the convicted woman would never show, but she appeared precisely at the appointed hour. She wore only a simple deerskin frock that came just above her knees and was sleeveless. Black hair hung free over her shoulders expect for a braid on the left side of her head, this indicated she was a virgin. Even common women in our kingdom shaved their legs nowadays, but hers were covered by a sheaf of black, curly hair. She walked barefoot. The soles of her feet were black, not from filth but from layers of callous—apparently she never wore shoes. She had large dark eyes, well-formed features, a sensitive mouth; quite a beautiful young maiden. I guessed her age at around thirty. The moment I saw her I knew would dismiss the charges against her. She knelt, clasped her hands, and bowed her head.

"Arise, maiden." She stood up gracefully. "You are called Sheena?"

"I am, my Queen."

"Sheena, I will hear the charges lodged against you"—I had already read them—"and hear your response to those charges. Then I will judge."

She nodded. I turned to the magistrate and had him read the indictment. He stumbled over many of the words. I think he was still in shock that the girl had showed up; and she had a presence that expressed purity, wisdom, patience, and devotion. There was something unsettling about her. She was beautiful in the manner of devoted women and exuded the dignity of the chaste and the calm of a woman intimate with holy things.

I won't go over the details. I think I've told you enough of them already. It did not take long for me to see the utter vacuity of the charges against her. And her response was articulate and measured. She spoke in a quiet, even voice. I remember, in particular, the ending of her defense.

"I am a simple maiden," she said. "I live in the woods and worship the goddess Freya, to whom I have dedicated my life and my virginity. I live in purity of devotion to her and do no harm. If I am to die for her name, I will embrace this as an honor. I trust your wisdom, Queen Elaine, and submit myself to whatever judgment you decree."

I contemplated, asked a few more questions, had the Council clarify some legal points, and then found in Sheena's favor. I also reprimanded the City Council and the priest who had brought charges against her.

"The accusation against this woman, and her condemnation, constitute a mockery of our laws," I said, my voice stern. The priest and the Council members looked terrified. "The Church of Saint Mark and the Council of this City will pay compensation to the Maiden Sheena for the time she was imprisoned and for the anguished and shame of being under a sentence of death. And the Council and the Church will issue apologies to her, which will be read in the public square at noon tomorrow." I looked at Sheena. "Is this acceptable to you, young woman?"

"It is acceptable, my Queen. I am, however, not allowed to possess money. If it might be given to the temple of my goddess, this would please my heart."

"It will be so." I glanced at the priest and the officials, who nodded, still in shock. I made a short speech in which I outlined the laws of our kingdom, talked about our toleration of religions other than our state religion, and assured all present that violations of non-Christian religions would not be tolerated. I did not want to be too hard on the Council, but I wanted to be clear where Oslac and I stood. The crowd listened. I caught looks of disapproval on a few faces, but many in the room showed expressions of surprised delight, satisfaction, and agreement with my words. I wanted the pagans to know we did not intend to harass or persecute them.

When I had finished, I looked at Sheena. She had stood for a long time and not moved or shifted from one leg to another.

"Sheena, I apologize to you," I said. "You are free to go. We will pay the amount of compensation—one-hundred gold crowns—to the Temple of Freya, as you requested."

"This is well, lady. Tomorrow I will worship there before returning to the woods. Will worship with us?"

I had to think fast, but it came to me.

"I am a Christian woman. I may not worship your goddess, but I will be honored to attend your worship, stand with you, and respectfully witness your devotions."

The Council and the Priest gaped. I gave them a look and they recovered their decorum.

"We will be honored," Sheena said. Then, with her peculiar graciousness, she knelt, clasped her hands, and bowed her head. I rose and left the room, summoning the Council to follow me.

I know now that I succeeded in reconciling the northern part of our land that day. In the months that followed my journey there, informers and spies we had hired told me how the enemy kingdom of Riata, on our northern border, a land that very much wanted to annex Wedmore, had sent agents provocateurs into our northernmost province. They used the incident with Sheena to stir the pagans in Wedmore to revolt. My exoneration of her defused the situation and riveted our pagan population's loyalty. At that time, though, I was not so sure it would all work out.

The next day, a huge crowd, many of them worshippers of Freya and Odin, turned out to hear the apologies of the clergy and city government. Sheena, wearing no cloak, barefoot and bareheaded in the cold and snow on the ground, and yet showing no reaction to wind and chill, stood beside the priestess of Freya and many of the Wedmore nobility who still worshipped the old gods. I made certain I honored and praised them, they had remained fiercely loyal to me during the revolt and had always supplied our armies with commanders and troops. The Council gave the hundred crowns to the Temple of Freya. The priest from Saint Mark's, who I knew to be a man of integrity, apologized for his behavior and asked Sheena's forgiveness for what he had done to her. She graciously accepted. All of this was tricky. I didn't want to turn the Christians of the province against me. The pagans' advantage in numbers made them a little nervous, I think, and they wanted to protect themselves. The way people embraced and greeted one another before and after the ceremony at least suggested some reconciliation had taken place.

I greeted Sheena, who introduced me to the Drudana, a woman of about fifty years, the Priestess of Freya. I met her husband and children. All the while we conversed Sheena watched me with her huge eyes. Being so near to her unsettled me. Her gaze seemed to look through me, not with hostility but with love and compassion. I felt a little wary, though, of someone so obviously invested in supernatural matters looking on me with the interest of affection.

Attending services at the Temple of Freya was the riskiest thing I did on that trip. I met with the leaders of the church and clarified my intentions, making certain they understood what I wanted to accomplish. They nodded, at first wanting to find fault with my action, but realizing, I discerned, that what I had agreed to was a good course to take.

"It will be as when Naaman the Syrian, who was healed by Elisha the Prophet and became a worshipper of the one true God, asked if he might still go into the house of the pagan god Rimmon—a thing required of him when he attended his King," I said. "Elisha permitted him to do so. We need to keep the peace in this province and to keep its people united. I am helping this effort by attending a worship service. I hope no one is so absurd as to think I would leave my faith for another. I am going to the Temple of Freya in a gesture of reconciliation. What was done to the maiden Sheena was unacceptable—I would even say it was provocative and foolish. We will leave it in the past where it belongs and move on from there. What I do this morning will be an important step in this direction. If anyone has advice for me, I will hear it."

The Superior of the fellowship of nuns in town, there were only three of them, not enough to have a convent, said my words were wise. The priest of Saint Mark's agreed. We all knelt in prayer and I went to the service.

It was a simple affair and in many ways similar to a Christian worship service. The congregation sang hymns of praise to Freya, prayed to her, and offered gifts of food and money to the support of the Temple. I offered blessing to many who asked for it and thanked Drudana for permitting me to attend. As I got ready to leave, Sheena approached me. After I bid her farewell, she leaned in close.

"Tonight," she said, "I will take you where your mother is." I could not reply and, after a moment, realized she did not want me to reply and had used magic to make certain I could not speak. "Go home and go to bed at the usual time you retire. I will come for you. No one will know."

After that I could move again. Sheena was gone. I did not see her vanish or any such thing. She simply was not to be found. I conversed with some of the nobility who were present. Drudana introduced me to her acolytes, two incredibly beautiful girls with golden hair and green eyes who were training to be priestesses. After much well-wishing and thoroughly sincere affirmations of loyalty by my subjects, I returned to my dwelling.

I spent the afternoon wondering if I had acted wisely, estimating the criticism I would get for sitting through a service at a pagan temple, and, most of all, wondering what would happen with Sheena. Her magical powers were considerable, I saw now, though I felt she would never use them maliciously. And she would lead me to my mother.

I met with my staff that afternoon. They had been diligent to gauge reaction to my all I had done the last two days here. Opinions were mixed, they said, but most of the people they spoke with thought I had acted wisely. I resolved to make certain I demonstrated Christian piety so as to offset any rumors I had become an apostate. I dined with the Mayor of the town, the nuns, and with Drudana, whom the Mayor had invited at the urging of the nuns. I thought this was a good sign.

Before retiring, I prayed with the nuns, Élodie, and my serving maidens. I slept with Cressida because I knew she slept like a log and would not awaken when Sheena came for me—though, of course, Sheena's magic would probably prevent that anyway.

Anxious as I was, I had had an exhausting day and fell asleep the moment I lay down. I felt someone touch my face and opened my eyes to see Sheena standing over me. She put a finger to her lips. I nodded and stood. I usually sleep naked, but tonight I had worn a smock. She motioned and I followed. We walked through the door to the bedchamber, but when we stepped out of it, we were in thick, darkness.

I could see nothing. I felt her take my hand.

"Come. This way. Let go of your fear."

I did the best I could and walked on a little easier. She held my hand but I could see nothing. I was not cold even though I knew I was walking in snow and felt the wind blow on me. After a while I saw a light, yellow like a fire. We drew closer to a simply constructed dwelling. The fire was one that burned outside its front door. By its light, I could see massive trees towering above me, snow beneath, and frost coating the underbrush that grew all around. Sheena spoke some sort of incantation, and gestured for me to enter into her dwelling place. I stepped through the door and found myself in a quiet, clean cabin, simply furnished. A table with two chairs sat in the center of it, a hearth with a small fire burning and cooking utensils hung around it took up one wall. In the corner of the room a small bed lay. On the opposite wall I saw an image of Freya.

Sheena bowed to the image and then turned to me.

"My home," she said.

"I'm privileged to be within its walls."

"Will you bless my home, Queen Elaine?"

"I don't know how the idea began that my blessing is efficacious."

"It is, I assure you—though not for the reason you probably think."

Feeling silly, I raised my hand. "My blessing upon this dwelling and upon the woman whose home it is. May this be a haven for her always, safe and secure; may she prosper in all that she does."

"Thank you."

"It is my privilege. May I know where my mother is?"

"She is laid to rest in a realm that may he entered only by magic. I will take you to her if you wish to go."

"Will the magic involved endanger my soul?"

She smiled. "The magic Alura did for you the night of the royal ball did not endanger your soul. It gave you a loving husband, the place of Queen, and your children."

I felt ashamed for what I had asked. Sheena sensed by distress.

"You need not fear. Your mother's magic could never be evil or harmful. She was too good to produce malevolent sorcery. I don't claim to be as good and wise as she was, but I try to follow her example."

"I'm ready to go to where she is."

"Come."

The wooden wall behind her bed had grown dark. She took my hand and led me forth. We walked past her bed and into the dark beyond it.

Time has a feel to it. I know this because that day I entered a place where time does not operate. I can't describe how it felt, but I was immediately aware that our world is a river that carries us forward in its current; the world into which Sheena led me was like a still, clear lake. Time rested here. In this realm, time did not flow but paused and gathered.

We walked on a path that felt like soft soil. A river ran parallel with the pathway. Black cliffs rose on the side opposite the river. The sky above glowed with moonlit clouds, though I could not see a moon shedding silver light. The river's murmur made the only noise I could hear. I saw no birds, no animals, and heard only the soft rush of the river. A length I asked Sheena where we were.

"There is a path that connects all things—every reality. People walk it but don't know that. You have the sight to see where you walk. Come long. Our destination is not much further on."

After another ten minutes we came to what looked like a small bay. Sand surrounded its margin. Rock rose out of the sand and formed natural steps up to a cave. I turned to ask why we had stopped. Sheena pointed.

"You will find what you desire up there."

I gazed at the dark mouth of the silent cave and turned to ask a question. Sheena was gone.

Fear set its ice on my soul. Had Sheena deceived me? Had I come under her power by entering Freya's temple and now would die or live forever in this world outside of time? My mind was like a place where two great rivers meet. Two massively strong currents of emotion churned my thought with strong, dangerous currents. Her abandonment had frightened me. But I wanted to see my mother. I looked up at the cave she had indicated. I climbed the uneven rocks to the entrance. I could see something inside glowing with dim, white light. I hurried inside. Lying on a square, sculpted stone lay a woman I assumed was my mother.

I approached and touched her face. Her flesh felt warm. I touched the side of her throat and felt a pulse. She was alive. Her chest rose and fell. Her hair, straw-colored like mine, fell about her shoulders. I felt I had met my twin. Well, maybe not a twin. I did not resemble her exactly, but the likeness radiated an image of me that I could not mistake.

She went away just after I turned five. That meant she had been here, under enchantment, twenty-three years, save the one night she appeared to me to bless me with her magic. I rejoiced but despaired. How could I break the enchantment? How could I wake her? And if I could not awaken her, how could I return to the world from which I had come?

Sheena was nowheere to be seen. She had abandoned me.

I looked down at Alura. I tried to think how I might awaken her. If Sheena did not return, awakening my mother would be the only way I would ever get out of this place.

I tried to remember anything Burnell said that might provide an answer. Nothing came to mind. Helplessness engulfed me like quicksand. I looked desperately about and then down at my mother's sleeping form—as if an answer might appear from one of those locations. Silence. I could not even hear the sound the river made. Once again, I touched her face. She did not react. I thought of gently shaking her, but that seemed like a violation.

Burnell had said she might be freed from one 'of her own blood,' but that did not seem sufficient to pull her out of the enchantment. I wondered if the term 'blood' should be taken literally. I thought I might cut myself and then cut her and mingle the fluid that life is in, hers and mine, but somehow that did not seem right either. If the spell had derived from evil fairies, it would be undone by something that would strike at their power. I could not see how my blood would do that, though I could think of no other course of action. I needed something with which I could cut myself and mother. A sharp stone? I glanced down at her.

She lay still, peaceful, lost in dreams. I marveled at the gentleness of her face. Here lay the mother I had hardly known—the woman who would have given me what I so craved growing up: love, affection, kind words, a gentle touch. Tears rolled out of my eyes and fell on her lips. Often in stories and tales, tears will free one ensorcelled, but mine availed nothing. I sighed. Perhaps, I thought, it was simply meant to be this way. Mother had not died. She looked peaceful. Perhaps selfishness moved my heart; perhaps she should not be awakened. I remembered seeing her that night when she used magic to give me a beautiful gown, a coach, footmen, serving maidens, and beautiful white stallions to pull my carriage. I remembered the fur slippers and my hair marvelously coifed. I could hardly see her in the dark that night. If I had, I might have remarked on how much we resembled each other. Before Alura appeared that night I had realized I would be a servant in Tremaine's house forever. When she died, Drusilla, the oldest and cruelest of the two sisters, would inherit me. I would probably never marry. I would live my life as a slave. Then Mother appeared and the sequence of my rise to the position of Queen began.

Such grace, I thought, must not be gainsaid. She probably used all her strength and all the magic she had left to deliver me that night. Did she temporarily break out of the enchantment in order to come to my aid and then fall into it again? If she lay at rest, what right did I have to slash at her flesh, to wake her, to enter a zone of dangerous magic, possibly endangering her? Blessing had flowed to me. I had a loving husband, dear children, and I ruled as Queen. I had friends and could use the wealth and power a monarch possesses to advance the common good of my people. As much as I crave her love and her touch, I told myself, it will be wiser not to disturb the repose she knows. I sighed and looked about for Sheena. I started to call for her when she appeared in front of me and stopped my mouth her hand.

"Don't shout," she smiled. She moved her hand away and. Sheena had beautiful white teeth which were not blemished.

I felt drained of strength. The struggle that made me decide to let my mother go on sleeping had been exhausting.

"You are virtuous woman, my lady," Sheena said.

"I hardly think so. I know my own heart."

"You just showed your heart. And you are correct in your musing. Your mother fell under this paralyzing spell. Your father thought she was dead—and, to him, she was. She had within her a little magic, knew what would happen to you, and, as she lay under enchantment, let that magic grow in a corner of her soul her captors could not see. Your mother broke the enchantment, did what she did for you, and fell asleep again. If she had not done the magic she did for you that night, she would not have gone sleep again. She could have rescued the life she knew before she was ensorcelled. But she loved you and sacrificed her desire so you could go free."

"Will she ever awaken?"

"The Council of the Good will awaken her. We had to know if she possessed enough strength to be brought out of the spell. We know she does because your thoughts were to give and not to take. This is Alura's nature, and its power of fills your soul. Hence, you behaved as she might have behaved. Her spirit in her and her spirit in you are one and the same. You are kind and loving, as she is, Queen Elaine. Being near her, your spirits flowed together. We know now we can awake her without causing her exhaustion or possibly her death. Come with me. The spell the Council must enact is complicated and takes several days to perform. But be assured your mother will return to you very soon."

I didn't want to leave her but knew I had to bow to the law of good that would awaken her.

Sheena led me along the soft dirt path by the river and the cliffs. We turned a corner and were break at her house.

I sat. She made tea and gave me coarse, rough but delicious bread and fresh cheese. We ate and drank.

"Thank you," I said when we had finished and she cleared. "You've been gracious."

"I must thank you, my Queen. You've been kind to my people—to the worshippers of Freya and of the old gods; and to me, since I would have been burned if you had not freed me."

"Do you like the life you live?"

She contemplated a moment, tilting her head back, looking up at the ceiling, and folding two fingers under her chin.

"That's an interesting question, and one I don't think I've ever considered. I love the life I have and love its freedom. I sometimes wonder if I would like to have a husband and children. But then there is the joy of being one with all that is, of not sharing my life, my time, my body, with anyone. The goddess gives me joy. The forest is a lovely place to live."

"You are a beautiful woman—beautiful in every way."

She brought out wine and told me about my mother. Through what she said I was able to understand her life, and mine.

My mother had been, like Sheena, a woman of the wood, dedicated to the old gods, possessing considerable magical powers. As Burnell had told me, though, she had enemies. Darkness invaded where she lived. Battles using magic, spells, and terrible incantations raged. Alura was driven from the wood. One rainy night, she sought refuge at an inn. The innkeeper told her to get out, but my father spoke for the wet, cold woman in a simple frock, barefoot, hungry, and exhausted. He arranged for her to have a meal and a room. That night Alura shaved for the first time ever, washed, smoothed her hair, and conjured a beautiful dress, soft leather shoes, and jewelry. In the morning she came downstairs as my father prepared to leave. Like all the people eating breaking that morning, he was stunned at her transformation and not a little taken with her.

"Regard me as a friend," he said, not wanting to be forward with her in front of so many people.

"Perhaps someday I will visit your borough," she replied.

Sheena said, "To make the story simple, she visited and they fell in love. Like me, your Mother had dedicated herself to the goddess, but the goddess appeared to her and released her from her vow. They were married. You were born. Your mother rejoiced.

"I wish I could say the story ended there. The Evil Ones had not given up. They knew your mother's magic excelled theirs, so they attacked you and your father.

Alura blocked their spells, but protecting both of you took a great deal of her power, and eventually they were able to overcome her. Painfully, you know the rest of the tale."

We were quiet a long moment. I looked at her in the flickering firelight, her appearance gentle as earth or sky, her loveliness the loveliness of nature itself.

"You are a worthy woman," I said.

"I am a simple maiden. Come. I will return you to your world."

Home was not far. Sheena opened a door; I stepped through it and was in my bedchamber. She did not follow me. I heard Cressida snore. All else was quiet. I stood a moment, head bowed, and climbed into the warmth and comfort of the coverings.

****

I journeyed back to the capitol. My trip to the Temple of Freya had caused some concern, but most people knew my commitment to the main faith in our kingdom, and I was careful, as often as I got the chance, to explain what I had done and why I did it. Our kingdom had worshippers of the old gods in most of our main towns; Jews lived in the capitol and in other areas of our kingdom. Both groups showed loyalty to the crown, and I think the people of our land realized this. My action in Wedmore ended up causing consternation among the sour, the pious, and the self-righteous—but those types of people feel consternation about almost everything anyway.

Winter turned to spring. Riata launched a surprise attack on Wedmore—or at least they thought it would be a surprise. Prophetess that she was, Sheena foresaw the attack and informed one of her uncles, who passed the word on to us. Our army lay in ambush when the Riatans made their foray into our land. We captured their king and commanding generals. No one was killed because our troops suddenly appeared in force all around them and they were sensible enough to surrender without a fight. We exacted tribute from them and forced them to annex their southernmost province, possession of which gave us control of a strategic pass that, once secure, made future invasion from Riata impossible.

At the victory celebration, Sheena gave me a sealed envelope.

"Open this when you return home," she said.

My fingers itched to see the message, but I restrained myself. Once home, I attended victory celebrations, receptions, and services of praise and thanksgiving that the kingdom had escaped invasion. After a week, I put the children to bed, kissed Oslac goodnight, he said he would come to my chamber on Friday for some sport, a thing I was eager for myself. I bathed, put on a smock, sent my serving maidens into the next room and broke the wax on the message. I read the following:

Elaine, my child. Come to me. I dwell in the house beside Giles' Winery.

----Alana

I summoned Cressida and another trusted serving maiden, Rebecca; ordered a guard of four soldiers, and rode out into the dusk.

Warm air blew on my face as we rode at a trot. Days had grown longer and light lingered in the sky. When we came to the winery, I dismounted and told Cressida and Rebecca to wait at the door. I had the guards post themselves a little way off, knocked on the door, and waited.

The door opened. A girl of probably thirteen years opened it, bowed, and took me inside. We passed through an anteroom and then into the main chamber. A fire burned. My mother sat in a rocking chair beside the hearth.

I started to speak but words would not come out of my mouth. I quickly realized I was growing smaller, shorter in stature and more diminutive. This might have frightened me, but at the same moment it began to happen I realized why it was happening and my heart filled with unspeakable wonder and joy.

As I grew smaller, the garment I wore collapsed in folds about me. The servant girl quickly pulled it away. By that time, my knickers and the linen bra I wore had fallen off. Just as well on the bra, because my breasts were gone. I found myself in the body I had at five years old. The serving girl pulled a cotton smock over my head. I slipped my arms into the sleeves, and stepped out of my shoes and hose.

My mother nodded. The servant girl gathered my garments, shoes, hose, and underwear, and then bowed, and left.

I stood, looking exactly as I looked at age five; dressed in the kind of smock I had worn to bed then. Mother smiled.

"You know what this is about, don't you Elaine?"

I nodded and voice choked with emotion, said, "Yes, Mother."

"Come to me, as you always dreamed you might."

I put my arms out, rushed to her, and climbed into her lap. She enfolded me in her arms, kissed my hair, and began to rock me.

I wept quietly. Of all the ways in which Mother might have greeted me; of all the gifts she might have given, this was what I had wanted more than anything, though I had not recently thought of it and had not imagined it would ever happen. As a child, and even as young woman, I had imagined a moment when my mother would sit me on her lap, tenderly hold me, kiss my hair, and rock me. I had dreamed of how I would rest secure in her love; how I would feel the warmth of her nearness.

Nights when I lay on my bed of reeds by the hearth, exhausted from work, lonely, miserable from the insult, taunts, and mockery of my stepmother and stepsisters; hungry and dirty; despairing and, like any other child, wanting to be cherished, I would imagine sitting on my lost mother's lap in a rocking chair by a warm fire. I would imagine her holding me and loving me. I would imagine how sweet and beautiful that would be. I envisioned warmth and sanctuary. Many nights I drifted off to sleep with this picture in my mind. I imagined it even when I grew into womanhood. I went to sleep with this vision in my mind the night mother came to transform me so I could attend the royal ball.

And now the dream had become reality.

I felt the joy of it go down to the core of my soul as I rested in that space I thought in my youth would be like heaven—and it was. I felt the warmth of the fire and the gentle rocking. I felt her breath on my neck and cheek, her gentle touch; and, above all, I felt love radiate from her. Is love not what we want above all else?

For a long time we did not speak. How many people, I pondered, are given their dearest dreams? I had married a strong but gentle man, became a Queen, and bore children—things I known in my fantastical thinking but never thought would come about. That was my first dream. Now, the deeper dream had come as well.

After a while, Mother said, "When you are ready, I will return you to your adult body. For now, rest in your dream."

"It is healing to my soul," I murmured.

"To mine as well," she said.

There would be much to talk about when she returned me to womanhood. For the moment, though, I rested as a child. What woman sees her greatest wishes granted and then gets to grow up a second time?

I lay there, curled in my mother's embrace. Outside, the spring night waned.

Spell Weaver

By Matthew Wilson

Tap - tap - tap, went the old witches stick as she came out of the cave. "What do you mean it isn't working out?"

Cinderella fixed her dress that had torn in the twigs. Since she'd escaped the house of her step sisters, she'd always hated ugliness. It reminded her of the dark past she wished to fully escape. She'd almost gotten away from all that -- she was married to a king for crying out loud. Even though she no longer loved him.

"I need another spell," Cinderella said, finally. "Something to kill Philip without throwing suspicion on me."

The old witch gave the matter some consideration, and seeing no humor in Cinderella's eye wondered what had happened to the bubbly newlywed she'd seen last. "There has to be another way, dear. Can't you save the marriage? The lad's always been so charming."

"I can't divorce him," Cinderella said, stamping her foot and crushing a beetle. "I'll lose the castle and the kids. I know he's seeing someone else. People laugh at me at court -- it's worse than living with my step mother."

The old witch shook the spiders from her hair and insisted that things couldn't be as bad as all that.

"You need more confidence, dear. I know you may have a little paranoia complex after the horrible things your step mother did to you -"

"I don't have a paranoia complex," Cinderella interrupted unkindly. "Who told you I did? Was it Charming's mother? She's never liked me, I read it in her diary."

"But you've had your wishes, dear. You had your happy ending --"

"But I'm not happy," Cinderella insisted. "Now are you going to help me? Or do I have to take matters into my own hands again?"

The old witch thought she'd saved Cinderella from evil. But now she saw she had spent too long under her step sisters' spell. Lacking confidence and suffering daily mental abuse, she'd become warped and distrustful. She couldn't see the good thing she had for the certainty it could not be real.

There was no such thing as happy endings.

She should try living in a cave, the old witch thought, disliking this stranger she'd once known as happy and beautiful. The years of worry had been unkind to Cinderella. Her hair had greyed and her eyes had lost that sparkle.

King Charming deserves better than her, the old witch decided. Silly girl doesn't know when she has it good.

"Well?" Cinderella demanded. As queen, she expected people to answer her right away. No more was she second fiddle to ugly sisters. People noticed her and if they didn't; she used her royal powers to make them. Her step mother had taught her the beauty of fear. The purest of weapons.

It got the job done.

"Very well, dear," the old witch said finally. "I'm your fairy god mother and it's my duty to make you happy."

"You're damn right," Cinderella said and followed her into the magic scented cave and wrinkled her nose like she'd stepped into something unpleasant. "God. How do you live like this?"

"Some people below the bread line have no choice, dear," the old witch said bitterly. This spoilt brat had never cried herself to sleep with hunger pains. She hadn't had to sell her clothes to afford food and eaten what rats she'd killed.

Not since the old witch had saved her from that awful house.

I have lived too long, thought the old woman. And made too many mistakes.

"Hurry. Is this going to take long?" Cinderella said, smacking aside some first edition hardback books from a chair but didn't dare sit down. She was no longer that sweet girl who got dusty. Now she made demands and expected them to be fulfilled immediately.

The old witch fixed her glasses and retrieved a blue bottle from off a shelf. "Here, dear. This will help you see into the hearts of men. If you want proof of Charming's infidelities, then --"

"Gimme!" Cinderella said and snatched it out of her hands.

"Careful, dear. You only need a drop."

"Shut up, witch. Matters of a Queen aren't your business any longer," Cinderella popped off the cork lid and drank half the contents in a single greedy gulp.

Now she had him. She'd unmask that charming villain as an adulterer and throw him out of her castle. She would keep her jewels... and her kids.

"You'd better not tell anybody about this," Cinderella warned. A Queen had to keep her secrets. "They used to burn witches in the old days and if your breathe a word--"

She stopped speaking when she realized the witch was growing. No, it wasn't that. Cinderella was shrinking! Her hands wrinkled and her back hunched. Her tongue shriveled, removing her scream and her vision dimmed.

Still though, she saw the remnants of her beauty flow from her like mist and attach itself to the witch. The old woman's back straightened, her walking stick dropped to the floor as white lightning moved through her dusty bones, rejuvenating them with new life.

The transformation took seconds and the old witch giggled like a girl when she wore a Queenly face and pushed Cinderella to the floor. Cinderella's bones were old now and she had no strength to remain upright.

"No. What have you done!" Cinderella screamed and the old witch thought that was obvious.

"Charming deserves someone better than you, dear. Try and return to our palace and see what the ramblings of an old witch will get you. Maybe they'll burn you like you threatened to torch me."

The old witches mouth worked but Cinderella could make little sense of her words.

"Our?"

"I'm sick of this wet cave," the old witch said. "You can be as ugly on the outside as you are on the inside and call this tomb, home."

Cinderella tried to stand but her body had suffered years of abuse and couldn't move well. "Wait -- you were supposed to make me happy!"

The old witch picked out a sweet hat and fixed it on her soap smelling hair. It was a little grey here and there but retained enough gold to catch a kings eye. "I promised to make Cinderella happy and as I'm now you -- you'll agree, I've kept my word."

"Don't leave me like this!" Cinderella screamed but stopped when her old voice box throbbed with agony.

"Take your time, dear," the old witch said. "You're not as young as you used to be. You have to slow down if you're going to live out here. It's a dangerous place for an old woman like yourself."

Laughing, the old witch headed outside, toward the new castle with her new body.

Toward home.

Inspired By

The Frog Prince

The Iguana Prince

By Rhema Sayers

"Listen, Tanya. You're not going to believe this. I mean I don't believe this and it happened to me!" I switch the phone to the other ear and open the refrigerator. "First off, here's this gorgeous hunk, who appears in my office as my last potential client for the day. He says he really needs a lawyer and not just any lawyer, but the very best. Therefore he needs me, since I am the best civil lawyer in the city. But I'm telling you, he was so goddamn good looking – we're talking movie-star looks here – that he was distracting."

I pull out a carton of skim milk and raid the freezer. Sorting through a stack of Jenny Craig dinners, I pick out grilled salmon and asparagus and pop it in the microwave after peeling off the cover.

"No - not just distracting - riveting! You know how I like to watch my client's eyes when he's telling his story, so that I can tell if he's lying? I couldn't do that. I'd look into those deep blue eyes and every thought in my head would disappear. I mean gone – poof – nada! I found myself leaning over my desk, inches from his face, lost in the azure pools of his eyes – drowning!" I squirm a little at the memory.

"And drooling."

The microwave dings and I pull out the dinner and cradling the phone between my shoulder and ear, juggle the hot food and milk into the living room. "Yeah – damn straight it was embarrassing! I'm hanging over him, spittle on my chin, and he's got this look on his face, like he's trying to decide if he can make it to the door before I go into heat."

Sitting on the couch, I grab the remote and flip the TV on. "I know - I turned flaming red. Anyway I sit back behind the desk and concentrate on taking notes as he tells his story. But even then I'm having trouble listening because I wonder if those unruly black curls would feel as soft as silk and…I'm stealing glances…   Then I have to pull myself back to my seat again. And he's starting to make excuses for leaving and I have to do something, so I tell him that if he goes out that door, he'll regret it for the rest of his life. While I'm thinking about how much I'll regret it."

I flip through a bunch of channels and settle on the jewelry channel so I can moon over the rings and talk at the same time. "So I put a stranglehold on my hormones, lift my chin and look him in the eye and tell him to start over. And after a long pause, he does. I think he's been through this kind of female reaction before."

The busty blonde on TV is showing off a tourmaline ring, dark green, surrounded by peridots.

Gorgeous. The ring – not the blonde. "So he says that he doesn't think I'll believe him because his story is just too fantastic. I'm starting to go all googly-eyed on him again and I pinched myself to snap out of it." I write down the order number for the tourmaline and peridot ring.

"And then – you're just not going to believe this, Tanya – then he tells me that he has just escaped from an evil witch who was keeping him captive in a basement under her home in the foothills. But she has cursed him. The curse is that he has to spend half his time as an iguana." After chasing the last bit of salmon around the disposable container, I get up and toss the container and the asparagus in the garbage.

"Tanya – Tanya! Stop laughing – I'm serious here. Well, yeah – I laughed, too. Hey – it's not that hilarious – calm down!" I click the TV off and start pacing back and forth. I'm beginning to regret calling Tanya. "Look – there I am – staring at this absolutely sumptuous man who has just classified himself as seriously mentally ill. So to give myself some time to think, I ask him why does he need a lawyer."

"Yeah, yeah – I know – he needs a psychiatrist more than a lawyer – or at least that's what I was thinking at the time." I wander into the bedroom and flop on my bed, kicking my heels off. "Well – get this – it seems that he's a prince from the ruling house of Montenegro – a Knjaz actually – he said it differently – I can't pronounce it. But the ruling house hasn't been ruling for about a century. Anyway according to Danny – that's the hunk – the evil witch wants to take over the world and she's starting with Montenegro. Danny says that as far as he's concerned, she can have it. He also says that he thinks she's going through menopause because of the incredible hot flashes she's having. But he's got to get out from under this iguana life and he's tried everything he can think of – wizards, witches, magic potions and wands. Nothing has worked.

And the last attempt simply landed him in her basement as a prisoner. So now he's going to take her to court. And he wants to start with a restraining order.

I roll over and stare out the window at the rolling hills and the city. "Anyway I'm so tantalized by this time that I would do almost anything to find out if this guy is as beautiful in bed as he is in my visitor's chair. But he's certifiably crazy and I'm trying to remember if I have my shrink's number on speed dial when he tells me how large the retainer will be."

The memory of the moment sends a thrill through me. "So we discussed finances for a few minutes. He's starting to look a little ill – breaks out in a sweat – turns a little green. And I'm wondering if he's actually good for the retainer, when he jumps up and races to the door, then back to my desk and then to the door – he does this three or four times, then scrapes at the rug with his shoe, turns around a few times and lies down in the middle of the rug, curled up in a fetal position."

I sit up and start rubbing my feet. "So I'm standing, leaning over my desk with my mouth hanging open and saying a silent goodbye to that retainer, when I notice that he looks funny. What? Yeah – funnier than curled up in the middle of my rug." I get up and go into the bathroom and rummage in the drawer next to the sink, coming up with Flaming Puce nail polish and sit on the side of the tub.

"The guy is shaking a lot and he's looking greener every moment. I'm reaching for the phone to call 911 when I notice that his face is changing! He's getting really ugly with warty things growing out and his eyes are protruding and a few minutes later I have a very large, wart covered green lizard in the middle of my rug instead of the studly prince."

I carefully put cotton puffs between my toes and start to apply the polish. "What? No! No, I haven't been using any drugs. I gave that up years ago. What's that smell?"

A vile odor has wafted in from the living room, mingling with the scent of the nail polish. "Hang on, Tanya. Something smells really bad."

I walk out into the living room and shriek "Danny! No!!!! Bad boy!!!! Noooooo!!!!!" I wail, forgetting that I still have the phone at my chin. "Ok, ok! Sorry, Tanya! Stop shouting! The fuckin' iguana just shit all over my Persian rug!"

I whap Danny on the rump and shove his warty nose in the direction of the bushel sized poop.

He slinks off into a corner and buries his face in his tail, back to me.

Grabbing Windex and paper towels, I get down on my hands and knees with the phone still propped between chin and shoulder. "Gross! You have no idea how much shit a seven foot long iguana can produce."

"What? Well, he's the same size as he was as a man. But he's got a tail, too." I use a spatula to shovel the poop off the rug and into a garbage bag.

"Anyway I haven't gotten to the point of this conversation. I'm not violating attorney-client privilege you know."

"Yeah. I thought you'd have that part figured out. I want you to start checking out the witch. Her name's Esther Hardcastle. I'll text you her address. We are going to take her down, as well as take her for everything she has." I take the rug out and hang it on the balcony railing. "We are going to force her to reverse the iguana spell so that my sweet Danny boy will revert to his Adonis form and we'll both be happy. Besides I think he might have trouble accessing his funds in this state. What? Hell, yes! That's an important consideration."

Danny comes over to me, eyes sad, tail hanging down. I relent, patting his head. The huge tail thumps on the floor. "That noise? That's Danny wagging his tail. I'm petting him." I gag. "Don't be disgusting, Tanya!"

Heading into the kitchen, I put away the Windex and paper towels. I'll have to get professionals in tomorrow to clean the rug. Or - on second thought - maybe I'll just take the rug to them. Explaining a lizard as big as a Komodo dragon in your condo will not be easy.

I continue giving instructions to Tanya. "He says he's exhausted the magical possibilities. Hmm? The kissing a frog option? Well - I actually tried that. You would not believe how foul iguana breath is. And the kiss didn't work. He told me earlier that he usually reverts to human in a few hours. So we'll discuss it further when he regains his senses and his body. His gorgeous body... mmmmm."

Walking back into the living room, I notice that Danny is sitting up, looking a lot less green and his eyes are not protruding any longer. I grin. "Well, gotta go, Tanya. Let me know what you find out. Yeah... that's right... talk to you later."

Inspired By

Little Red Riding Hood

Kel Shot

By Evelyn Wilbur

She dreamed.

The mist hung lazy in the woods, clearing only to reveal the dark path before her. She carried a basket. Always a basket. Forest sounds filled the darkness, but other more sinister sounds were hidden beneath them. Each treacherous step along the path was a test of her courage. As the path itself threatened to crumble and break apart beneath her, plunging her into a deep abyss from which she could never return.

A howl rose in the night and shadows moved just beyond the tree line. Yellow, glowing eyes followed her progress along the path. Running footsteps behind her caused her to spin around. But the path was empty. Hot breath on the back of her neck chilled her and as she turned the wolf's face materialized in the blackness. The scream that rose in her throat was swallowed by the wolf as it lunged with wide open jaws and teeth that glistened in the moonlight.

She awoke.

As the dream faded into the fog clinging to the land, she sipped at her coffee allowing the bitter liquid to warm her. The lazy sun began to stretch across the property, awakening everything it touched, including her. She wrapped her thick, tattered, neon-green bathrobe tighter around her and stretched her neck side-to-side like a boxer preparing for a title fight. Her ex-boyfriend always said the robe made her look like the Wicked Witch of the West. She couldn't help but feel like it were a loyal old friend and she was especially attached to the black half-moon patch on the pocket that hung on by two stitches.

Since moving in, her photography career had bloomed and sleeping in was a forgotten luxury. It became essential after her Grandmother died for her to keep busy so the grief wouldn't surround and suffocate her.

Only three days ago she'd decided to clear her calendar for today; though she had been planning for it her whole life. Most of her clients were little girls between three and eight years old, whose temper tantrums were only upstaged by their over controlling parents. But today, that could all be pushed behind the curtain and she could design her own fantasy world. And in that world there were lazy coffee drinking mornings, and it was heaven.

In the back of her mind she also knew in this moment of introspection it was time to stop running from the grief. She was ready. She was tired of feeling broken and lost. It was time to be happy. Really happy and not this fake façade she built around herself. Kel had grown comfortable with hiding behind things; a hood, a camera lens, behind the shadow of a redwood forest.

Gulping the final drops of coffee, Kel thought back to the howls from the wolves last night. The pack's sweet chorus had disturbed her sleep, as it often did, but she sympathized with their cries. As a child she'd visited her Grandmother here at this cabin often and it was here her fascination with the wolves began. Her Grandmother had lived in harmony with the animals and had encouraged Kel to respect their wild power.

When she was a teenager she'd found a wolf pup struggling and whimpering. He was caught in a fishing net. Kel ran into the cabin to get scissors and untangled the puppy. The poor thing whimpered the whole time but didn't fight her or try to bite. At one point he even licked her hand as if to encourage her further. To her surprise he didn't run when she freed him. He only stood there staring at her. The wolf looked deep into her before slowly turning and walking away, with several slow and deliberate steps before bolting into the forest. That's when she noticed the white patch of fur behind his right ear, a half-moon shape.

Entering the house, the old swinging door creaked loudly, it was the sound of a hundred summer days, each moan a memory from her childhood. She placed her favorite coffee cup which read: COFFEE. Because it tastes better than fiber. - in the sink. Before showering, she grabbed from the shelf in the hall a wolf book her Grandmother had given her. It was one of her dearest treasures.

"Remember, out there is the beast's domain and playground." The old woman would remind her grandchild." They see you as the intruder and they will always pounce to protect it."

Her grandmother would often play along with her when she pretended she was red riding hood. When Kel was ready to play she would get her basket and tie a red and white checkered table cloth around her petite neck.

"Grandmother would you give me some sweets for my basket?" Tiny Kel asked.

"Where are you going with the sweets?" her grandmother asked.

At five years old she had rewritten the fable to fit her imagination. "I'm taking them to the wolf." Kel said gleefully.

"But what about the big ears?" Grandmother asked.

"The better to hear me coming with the treats." Kel squeaked in excitement.

"And what about the big eyes?"

"The better to see me with."

Grandmother tip-toed closer to Kel."And what about the horribly big mouth?"

"The better to smile at me with!"

Grandma always laughed at this exchange, which happened at least twice a week."Not the better to eat you with?" She'd cackle and chase Kel around the yard with sweets dropping from the bouncing basket.

A strange sound intruded on her memories and Kel heard creaking from the back porch floor boards. Pulling aside the blinds she caught movement at the edge of the porch and she glimpsed the tail of a wolf.

She froze.

Her heart pounded like a wild bird beating its wings on a cage door. She smiled without showing teeth and darted down the dark narrow wood paneled hallway.

Wildly swinging open the bedroom door she fumbled for her camera bag while tossing off the bulky robe.

Giving the digital camera a quick inspection, Kel slipped the strap over her right shoulder. From the closet, she grabbed a red cloak.

The cloak had been handmade by Grandma for her birthday fifteen years ago. Her Grandmother had sewn it large enough to grow into. The red fabric was as soft as moonlight with an oversized hood lined in the same material.

Flinging the cloak over the opposite shoulder, she grabbed the tripod from the closet floor. Twirling in her socks on the hard wood floors, she tossed the tripod over her shoulder and removed her baseball cap, hurling it towards the bed, missing and hearing it thump on the floor. Her long, black, curly hair exploded in waves framing her face and partly covering her left eye. Snatching the camera's remote control off the dresser, she sprinted for the porch.

Out the back door, she looked over the grounds. No sign of the wolf or its pack. The forest was still... too still. Sitting on the table where she'd had coffee earlier, she slipped on her black, shabby rain boots.

Bending over to pull on the last boot, Kel flipped her head up and hurriedly snatched her camera gear when, off to her left, leaves rustled softly.

"I'm nuts. I'm insane." Kel said out loud." But if I can pull off this shot... "

Several yards behind the house there was a flat clearing in the forest. Kel flung the heavy canvas sheet off the 1960's purple velvet love seat. Folding the canvas quickly, she placed it out of sight and began to set-up her equipment. The large airtight container remained where she had placed it the night before on top of the sofa cushions. The chicken blood and gizzards would be the insurance she needed to draw in the pack. She spread the contents quickly on the surrounding ground. Drips and splatters covering her boots. With everything ready, Kel put on the red cloak and sat on the sofa.

She'd used this sofa as a prop when photographing little girls dressed up like little red riding hood. The parents loved their daughter's pictures in the forest with giant baskets. It's what she had built her business around. What she was known for. But there had always been one picture she wanted more than anything. The shot of her dreams.

Using her remote control she fired off a few test shots and then sat and waited. She had never seen a wolf so close to the house since the pup. It was a good sign.

Every noise made her skin prickle. The air grew thick and heavy, and while the cloak kept her warm, she began to shake in fear. She was suddenly aware how isolated the cabin was. Danger could sneak up on her from any corner. It was, after all, the wolves' playground.

Kel often put herself in dangerous situations. This wasn't the first. Adrenalin was her favorite drug and she loved pushing herself to create portraits that moved people.

It didn't matter that she was an only child and had no boyfriend, husband, or boy-toy. That's how she liked it. Who really wanted gentleman callers? She wasn't a southern belle and this wasn't the nineteen forties.

Her widowed father had remarried and had a new instant family that she got updated on by yearly generic "how our family is doing" Xeroxed Christmas letters. She had let him know about her new photo projects but he showed little enthusiasm. He had always wanted her to be a dentist so she could take over his practice when he retired. But the idea of working the rest of her life in other people's mouths wasn't going to feed her need for adventure.

If she could get this picture it would be the missing piece to getting a large gallery showing in the city. A real chance to exhibit all she had done. The risk was worth it.

She had to try and charm the beast.

Fifteen minutes passed since she had seen the wolf on the porch. Still she sat frozen. She was prepared to stay all day if needed. She had planned to do this today even before she saw the wolf. That's why last night she had buried five bloody rags close to the house, hoping the scent would draw in a wolf. And it had worked.

A cluster of birds exploded from the treetops nearby. Kel drew in a deep breath and held it. She had a vision of the picture she wanted. She would be sitting on the sofa with her face in profile looking at the wolf. The hidden remote control would fire off the camera set on rapid fire, capturing the wolf in frame with her. She knew it wouldn't be as easy as it sounded. Nothing in life ever was.

From the right she heard swift stomping against the ground, unsure if the sound was coming towards her. She knew in the forest sounds don't always travel in a straight line.

Kel dried her sweaty palms and repositioned the remote control in her right hand. From this angle it wouldn't be caught in the picture and that was important.

Excitement and fear rose to a thunderous beating of her heart. "It's really going to happen!" she thought.

Kel adjusted her cloak. She wanted just the right amount of hair peaking from under the hood. She'd been disappointed before but not today. Today would be different.

Out of the corner of her eye she saw movement. Her mouth was dry. Her heart screamed in her chest. Here was the moment that would define her life or end it. Either way, this would be the end to her fairytale deep in the woods.

Quickly the grey blur came into focus. Only a few feet from Kel a pack of six wolves charged from the forest. Her breath caught in her throat. She sprung off the sofa, engulfed in fear. She could use the tripod as a weapon. But her feet wouldn't move. The wolf pack was closing in too quickly. There was no time to waste.

Dropping to her knees in front of the couch, she forced her trembling limbs to move. Stretching out her arms in a welcoming gesture, she hoped her camera would capture her coaxing them forward, taming the beasts. Her thumb was on the remote. She had committed herself even though her trembling limbs told a different story.

A painting she once saw at a museum flashed in her mind, a maiden in white in this same position with arms extended just about to touch a white palomino horse. She would get this shot. Though it might be her last, it would be her best. She pressed the button and heard the shutter snap off five clicks.

The pack noticed Kel and stopped before they were in frame. Every head in the pack turned toward the camera. With teeth gnashing, and barking wildly they circled around each other but kept their distance.

"Come a few inches closer." Kel whispered with a quivering voice. "I won't harm you."

The pack sniffed the air. Suddenly the largest wolf lunged and Kel pressed the button. Hurriedly she swung both arms in front of her defensively like a baseball player swinging an invisible bat, knocking the animal to the side. The wolf's body slammed the camera to the ground with a crash. Swiftly, Kel grabbed a sofa cushion and used it like a shield as the second wolf charged. The animal tore into the cushion and whipped its head like a puppy playing with an old rag, wrenching the cushion out of her hands. The rest of the pack circled the sofa at top speed.

Kel, still on her knees and now unprotected, watched as the second wolf jumped on top of the sofa. Snapping at the air the creature pulled back his head and howled. Her mind commanded her to run but before Kel could stand, the lead wolf charged again, knocking her onto her back. Kel closed her eyes, screaming in anticipation. Any second now she'd feel the wolf's powerful jaws ripping at her throat. But the bite never came. The wolf's bared teeth stopped inches from her neck. He barked close to her ear and smelled her scent with his massive paws pinning her to the ground.

Kel forced her eyes open and the forest around her glowed in a white hazy light. The beast stared down at her, while flickering beads of dust imitating tiny fireflies danced and floated around between them. Immediately she felt the familiar connection. As if this wolf were not only linking to her soul but mending it as well. Time and space no longer existed. It was just the two of them in this moment. Could this be the same animal she rescued so long ago? Could this be the puppy? The wolf licked her sweaty neck, and the roughness of the tongue irritated her skin. Even though she smelled metallic blood mixed with musky soil on the wolf's breath, she wasn't afraid. Before she could speak, before she could even form a thought, a shotgun blasted overhead and time rushed back from its angelic state.

The pack scattered and the large wolf leapt off Kel's chest, but not before she saw the half-moon patch of fur behind the ear.

A young man yelled, "Miss, are you alright?"

Kel rolled over onto her side, looking at the camera on the ground. It didn't appear to be damaged.

"Yes." She could barely get the small word out. She had temporarily forgotten how to speak.

The stranger came closer and knelt beside her. "Are you hurt?"

Kel could smell the thick scent of gunpowder lofting all around. The stranger placed the shotgun along-side her and looked out at the forest. He was an angel dressed in camouflage pants and a light brown corduroy jacket.

"I've been tracking this pack." he said, "They killed some rabbits on my farm down the hill. I was concerned when I heard you scream. Didn't think I'd make it in time."

She took the out-stretched hand but her legs buckled.

"Bambi legs," Kel said busting into a nervous giggle. "Maybe I should sit on the love seat before I try to walk?" Kel looked behind her. "Do you think we're safe?'

"Yes. Let me help you." He gently guided her to the sofa.

Sure that she was going into shock, Kel sat for a few moments, silently trying to fight off the uncontrollable shakes.

"My name is Hunter. What's your name?"

"Kel. Thank you for saving my neck." She looked down and saw a large rip on her cloak. "And the rest of me too."

"Sure thing." He chuckled, "Nice cape."

"Thanks." Kel said, not sure if he was poking fun. "It's hard to find something that goes with my rain boots."

Hunter's unexpected laughter filled the clearing. Kel was glad for that sound. It helped her nerves.

"Can you help me to the cabin?" Kel asked.

"Sure. Are you ready now?"

"I'm as ready as a condom on prom night." Stunned at herself, Kel's cheeks flushed in embarrassment. "WOW! Did I just say that? I swear you didn't just save a crazy lady. I'm completely harmless. Maybe a little nuts, but harmless."

Kel pointed over Hunter's shoulder. "Can you grab my camera for me?"

He hadn't noticed the camera until now.

Puzzled Hunter asked, "What were you doing out here?"

"If you have time, I'll explain over coffee." Kel locked arms with Hunter.

"Well since you're only a little nuts, sure why not."

Old Granny's Skin

By Cheresse Burke

The cottage is dark. I'm not sure how I feel about that, in my current condition. On one hand, I never minded the dark. It was more of a friend to me than daylight. Darkness is comfortable. But I'm also in a closed space, and that's not to my liking at all. A Wolf like me needs to breathe, to smell the pine and the dirt and the mice and foxes and rabbits and all their little decaying houses, the stench of fear in the prey as she streaks through the night, leaving a bright trail for me.

Squeezing into these tight spaces is a matter of cunning, and that's more Coyote's business than mine. He put me up to it. "Squeeze into old Granny's skin," he said, "and you'll get the tastiest meal of your life."

Coyote's known for tricking people. This probably should have occurred to me earlier. But the way he said it, he sounded so convincing. I could almost feel her bones between my teeth, crunching sweetly. So of course I agreed.

I'm in the skin but Coyote's doing all the talking. I can't even move around in here, for fear I'll rip the thin façade and reveal the fur beneath. All I can do is open and close my little Granny mouth, like I'm trying to say something. And I'm only allowed to do that when Coyote speaks.

Lying here on my back feels wrong, too. I'm exposed. Just one huntsman with his axe...   you hear about cases like that. The old Granny trick, it's been tried so many times now that I can hardly believe I'm giving it a go myself. What if the little girl has a knife, or even a gun? Kids these days aren't as innocent as they used to be.

"Footsteps on the path!" Coyote whispers. He's hiding under the bed. "Are you ready?"

I can't say anything, but even if I could I'd tell him it's too late now. I have to stifle the growl, and the desire to go for his throat. My belly itches, but if I reach down to scratch it, I'll rip the skin. My claw almost pierces old Granny's fingertips anyway. Damn Coyote and his schemes. "We'll split the body, fifty-fifty," he said to me. As if his fine talking is worth fifty percent of the meat! No matter. After she's spilled on the floor, we can renegotiate the deal.

"Just stay calm," Coyote murmurs. Easy for him to say. My eyes roll around of their own accord, and I curse myself again. If she looks into my eyes the game will be up for sure. We had to pluck out old Granny's in order for the skin to fit properly. They didn't taste too good, either. Too many cataracts.

I'm so vulnerable, lying like this. Trapped under a foreign skin and an old nightgown. And what if it's not her? What if it's the woodsman, coming to see if old Granny's all right? What if it's soldiers who want to ransack the place? I haven't seen much war in these parts, lately, but you can never tell when a soldier's going to decide that his adventuring time has come, and wander off into the woods to start saving little girls and killing hapless, innocent wolves.

A scrape sounds at the door, and it creaks open. My heart lifts a little. Just a girl. Easy prey. Tender under her coat, I imagine.

"Hello, Granny," she calls as she shuts the door. I can see the dark form of her coat, and smell the wet wool. I hate chewing through wool. I hope she takes it off before we spring.

I open and close my mouth. Coyote says, "Hello, my dear." He's done the old coat-your-throat-with-honey trick to make his voice sound sweeter. But he still sounds like a tree, creaking in the wild wind.

"Oh, you don't sound good at all," she says, and starts to move about the cabin. "Why don't we get a little light around the place?"

"No," Coyote says, a little too quickly for me to get the mouth working. "No, my dear. I can't stand the light. I'm becoming sensitive in my old age, you know."

"Come on, Granny. A little bit of sun won't hurt you."

My delicate nose, which has been muted by this cursed skin, finally picks up on the scents wafting from the bag she's brought with her. Fresh baked bread - blech. And something with cinnamon in it - not for me, cinnamon's nothing more than tree bark anyway. But smoked meats - venison, by the scent of it. My exposed stomach grumbles.

She moves to throw back the curtains, and something crunches under her feet. I can't see her form, from where I lie, and to twist and turn would risk ripping Granny's skin. But I hear her gasp. "Granny!" she says. "Your window!"

"Oh, that little thing," Coyote says. Can she really not recognize how different his voice is from the old woman's shrieks? "Not to worry. A couple of boys, playing baseball. The ball came right through here and they just ran off, didn't even say sorry. I wanted to find their parents but confined as I am... " he coughs pitifully.

"Oh, Granny," sighs the girl. "This is why we bought you a phone. So you can call us when something like this happens." She doesn't notice the tufts of fur around the window - I know they must be there because I can feel the scrapes on my sides and belly. But that's the magic of Coyote - when he says something, people believe him. He can make the hardest man a gullible fool. Maybe that's why his voice is worth half her meat.

Don't get soft, I tell myself. Coyote can slip among the houses and run along the highways. Coyote can dig through the trash. Poor old Wolf is trapped in the wilderness, dwindling as it is. Coyote can pay for the options he has.

"Well, I've brought you some soup, and bread from Uncle Yanni, and they had a special down at the deli on bison jerky and deer sausage. But don't eat too much at a time, you know your teeth don't do well with it."

"You're so good to me, dear," says Coyote. I lift one hand from the covers, just a little, as if I'd like to reach out to her but can't manage the strength. Inside, I feel Granny's skin shifting and creaking. In less than an hour it'll slough right off. Then the game will be up, no matter what.

She moves around in the little kitchen nook that sits in the corner of the cottage, bustling around, banging on pots and pans. I hear the click of the gas sparker and my heartbeat nearly cracks the Granny skin over my chest. Fire is no friend to the Wolf. I came down into the foothills to avoid the fires that sprang up deep in the mountains, feeding off the dead pines.

But she's not burning down the house, and she hasn't discovered our little game. She's only heating up the soup. I can smell potatoes and carrots. Disgusting. But I also catch the scent of beef broth, homemade.

"When I tell Mom about this, you know what she'll say," the girl calls as she stirs the soup.

"Yes, dear," says Coyote meekly.

"She's going to want to move you down to the flats. It'll be good if we can look in on you more than once a week. We can call the police if anyone tries to break in, or hits baseballs through the window. And we can even run you to the grocery store if need be."

"I like it out here," Coyote says. "Near to the wilderness."

"I know," she replies. "But maybe it's just a little too wild for you now."

She finishes heating the soup and spoons it into a bowl for me. I'm not sure how well I'm going to be able to eat as Granny, but I try to wiggle into a half-sitting position.

When she comes back over, I can see that she's taken off her coat. She's wearing a bright red, tight t-shirt underneath, and jeans that slide into her boots. Her belly pokes out between the line where her shirt stops and her tight jeans start. The sight sets my mouth to watering. She's not as insubstantial as so many city girls try to be these days. I open and close Granny's mouth expectantly and the girl begins to spoon soup into my maw.

"Do you want me to read to you, after?"

"Yes, please," says Coyote, while Granny still has a mouth full of soup. I don't think Red notices.

Red tries to hand me the bowl, but I make Granny's hands shake so much that she has to finish with the soup before she can pick up her book. The soup is barely digestible, thick with veggies and roots and hardly any meat in there at all. It makes me long for a good chunk of liver. Her liver. The thought helps me choke down the last of it, but I shake my head when she asks if I want any more.

Red picks up her backpack and pulls out a thick book of short stories. I can see Hans Christian Andersen stamped on the spine. I'm personally hoping that she'll read The Tinderbox. I have a soft spot for the three dogs in that one. They have something of the Wolf about them, even if they're only servants to man in the end.

Even wolves can get a little cultured, you know.

"I think we were in the middle of 'The Snow Queen'," says Red.

"Why don't you start from the beginning, dear? I've forgotten what happened," says Coyote. I quash the growl in my throat. Does he want us to be here all night?

Red doesn't seem to want to take it from the top, either. She summarizes what we've read so far and picks up around two thirds of the way through. Her reading voice is pleasant - I can feel my eyes drooping and I have to fight to stay awake. If I start to sleep, I might twitch and growl and whine and do all sorts of Wolf things. I focus on my belly. The soup has taken the edge off my hunger, but I can still feel it, just below my belly. The need for meat, the constant ache. As I study it, it grows, until I'm sure that I could eat her all by myself, and to Hell with Coyote.

After fifteen minutes or so, she sets the book down and reaches for one of Granny's hands. "Are you feeling better?" she asks.

"Oh yes," trills Coyote. "The soup's done a world of good, my girl."

"Good." She smiles, a tender smile a little like the one a mother might bestow on her cub. It bemuses me. Humans are such odd creatures, obsessed with tethering old ones to the earth, regardless of how dull and pointless their lives become. Is it better to let Granny waste away in bed than it is to let her go out with some kind of dignity?

Because even if I do justify this little game in my head, I can't admit that it's dignified for anyone involved. Now, Coyote doesn't give a rat's tail for dignity, and I can't speak for Granny. But wolves are supposed to be majestic. If my pack were here, they'd howl with laughter. But I was separated from them many mountains ago, and all my travels haven't helped me to find new pack mates. That's why I'm here, after all. I have to eat somehow.

Red pulls me out of my philosophical considerations when she takes Granny's hand and gasps. "You're cold as ice!" she cries.

I'm wearing Granny like a glove. Of course her hands are cold.

"Oh, don't worry about that, dear. You know these old bones aren't as quick to warm as they used to be."

But Red is concerned now. She runs her hands up my arm. "Your whole body's cold, Granny," she says. Her eyes narrow as she takes in my strange proportions for the first time. "And your arms are…long. Have they always been this long?"

"Of course, my dear. How else can I wrap them so well around you?" Coyote replies. He's trying hard not to do the 'All the better to' shtick. I can appreciate that.

I close my eyes in false exhaustion. I can't have her looking at them too hard. But she's squeezing the arm now, feeling out the bony knee of my leg stuffed through Granny's skin. "I think we should take you to see the doctor," she says. Her voice trembles as though she's trying not to panic. I can't help myself. I open my eyes to get a better look at her.

Big mistake. She's looking right into my face, and at the sight of my large pupils she starts back. Her mouth works, trying to find something to say. At last she settles on, "Have you eaten anything else today?"

"Oh, a little," says Coyote. "A little of this and a little of that."

Red gets up again and goes to fetch something from her bag. I get a good, full view of her ass in the process. I know it's all fat, but it reminds me how thin and unsatisfying the vegetable soup was.

When she turns back around, she's holding a cell phone up to her ear. Even through Granny's inferior ears I can hear the tinny voice of a man asking how she's doing.

"Fine," she says. "Could you drop by my Grandma's for a few minutes? I mean, if you're in the neighborhood." Her voice is higher when speaking to him than when speaking to Granny. And she's leaking pheromones.

"Okay," she says after a brief pause. "Okay. Thanks. Right, bye." Then she sets the phone down. "George is coming by, okay?"

"Any friend of yours, dear," says Coyote.

Red frowns. "Don't you like him? He does a lot for you, you know."

"Of course, of course. Why don't you read some more to your old Granny?" Coyote tries to cover for us quickly. I'm impatient for the game to be up.

Red looks at me for a long time, frowning. Finally she agrees, though she goes to the toilet first.

While she's gone I risk cracking Granny's jaw and open my mouth a fraction. "Now is the perfect time," I hiss in the direction of the floor.

"No," says Coyote. "No. I've got an idea."

I have a nasty suspicion. "We have to leave before her man gets here. We can't take both of them."

Coyote scoffs. "Of course we can. Humans are weak now. They lack their muscles and their heads have gone soft, looking at their computers and their papers and their phones."

"But we have to kill both of them. We can't let them get away and we can't let them scream. How are we supposed to do that, with just the two of us?"

"He'll be soft. That's how men are now. And just think, twice the meat...   " Coyote's sly voice is doing it again. I envision this George eviscerated on the floor, watching me eat his liver as he bleeds out the last of his life.

I have a thing for liver.

Red comes out of the bathroom, wiping her hands on her tight jeans. "Were you saying something?" she asks.

It's up to me now, at least I'm smart enough to get that. If I make the jump Coyote will have to follow. But the image of George follows me around, as if Coyote's still speaking with that magical voice of his.

She opens up and reads some more from 'The Snow Queen'. But she loses her place a number of times, glancing up. She's fixated on my body. I lie as still as possible, so as not to shift around too much in Granny's skin and cause an unwanted tear that could give the game away. Now that we've decided to wait for George, it wouldn't do much good if her screams alert him as he comes up the drive.

At long last we can hear him, crunching up the gravel. Red smiles a little too brightly and puts the book back in her bag. Then she hops up to get the door just as he knocks.

Two giant forearms push the door open, followed by a torso roughly the size of a barn. I can't help it, a whine escapes my throat and my tail starts thrashing around in Granny's back end, trying to get out.

If George is a weakling, then I'm a Chihuahua. He looks like he could kill me by stepping on me. The man stands at six foot four. I'm not sure whether he has to turn sideways to get through the door or just chooses to, but his shoulders are twice the breadth of a normal man's. His upper arms ripple with muscles the size of Red's head, and his legs are the legs of a runner. I'm afraid, for an instant, that even I couldn't outrun him.

He glances at me when I whine, but I'm pretty sure he doesn't see through the Granny disguise. But Red gives him a hug, and leans up to mutter something in his ear. Granny's loose skin blocks most of the sound but I get the words "not well" somewhere in the whispered conversation.

"Hi, Olive," he says, grinning. He's a clean shaven boy, and his teeth gleam whitely. It's not reassuring in the least, even though humans don't mean that sort of thing as a threat. "How are we doing today?"

"Oh fine, fine," says Coyote from under the bed. His voice has risen in pitch. Either he's applied more honey or he's seen our weakling George. I'm betting on the latter.

"You're looking a little... well, loose around the edges," he says. Not much of one to mince words, it seems. "Have you eaten much today?"

"We just had a bit of soup, but I was about to get some dessert out. What do you think, Granny?" Without looking at me, Red turns to go back into the kitchen nook. George follows her.

"I'm gonna shoot this season," he calls over his shoulder. "I can bring you a couple of venison steaks, if you've got the freezer space."

My tail thrashes so hard that Granny's skin twitches on the bed. The whine in my throat turns into a growl, and back into a whine. He's a hunter. I hate hunters. Even if they're not allowed to kill me, enough of them still take the shot.

"Olive?" He turns back around. "You okay?"

"Fine, dear, fine... why don't you come help an old lady up?" says Coyote. "I've been stuck in this bed long enough, and a fine man like you could help me walk about a bit.

That seems like my cue.

George comes over to the bed. His eyes start to take in what Red's been a little slower in piecing together. "You know, Olive, you look really... " He struggles to find the right words. "Have you seen a doctor lately?"

"Why should I?" Coyote is all petulance. My heart is trying to beat me to death. My claws scrabble at Granny's fingertips, start to shred the skin there. I'm past ready. I just want to go for the kill.

"Your eyes," he starts. "And your arms." He twitches the covers away from me. Sees the fat Granny skin stretched over my lithe frame. "Your... "

"It's no matter," says Coyote. His voice has turned to a growl. He's ready, too. "I feel fantastic!"

He leaps from under the bed, tackling George with a yowl. I spring up, trying to shake off Granny and get my jaw free and my claws ready and make the leap for his throat, all at once. But Granny's not so easy to get rid of as I supposed. I get tangled in the remains of her skin, even though it's papery and breaks apart with ease, and I flop off the side of the bed in a disgraceful heap.

I'm only incapacitated for a few seconds, but even that's too long. George had something that neither Coyote nor I could see, in our various positions. He was holding a bread knife when he came back to the bed.

Now, a bread knife isn't much. But when a man like George is wielding it, it doesn't need to be. He could probably pierce flesh with his bare hands. With his left hand, he seizes Coyote by his snapping throat. With his right, George drives the bread knife right into Coyote's guts.

Those aren't exactly the entrails I was imagining on the floor. And what's worse, the blood, the sudden stench of punctured intestines, reminds me what a fresh kill looks like. If I could have, I'd have stayed to snack, and that makes me feel more than a little disgusting. I mean, sure, Coyote's lower on the food chain than I am, but we're a pack, if just for this game. We were a pack.

Red nearly breaks my eardrums with her scream. Piercing isn't the half of it. We wolves have sensitive hearing in enclosed spaces. It'll probably take me a week to get my full hearing range back. If I survive at all.

She's still screaming but I can see that she's not totally witless. She rushes towards Coyote with a much bigger, sharper knife than the one George is holding. I don't really stop to figure out what kind of knife it is - sharp and pointy, that's enough for me. While Coyote's kicking and flailing and letting his guts flop on the floor, I high tail it, leap for the window we came in through and land about half in, half out. Excess glass that we failed to clear out of the pane grinds into my fur and punctures the skin in places, giving me little pinpricks of pain. No time to think about that now. I hear George shouting something like, "Get the other one!" and I scrabble for purchase with my back legs until I wriggle all the way out onto the ground outside.

Granny had a beautiful back garden, before we came along and trampled it. I dash past the tulip bulbs and upended piles of earth, through the gap in the hedge that we half-forced, have torn aside, and out into wilderness.

I can still hear shouting from George, screaming from Red. Coyote's blood is thick in my nose and fear like that of prey courses through me. In the distance, George says something. I can make out the words, "... get my gun... " and I pick up the pace.

Coyote was the trickster. Maybe he managed to trick his way out of death. But me, I'm the muscle of the operation. And my muscles are going as fast as they can, back to the safety of the mountains.

The first few miles fly by in blind panic. But when I've run out the worst of the fear, my concern starts to fade. Once I slow down to a trot, I stop making so much mess as I go, and I'm confident that George will give up after a few hours of fruitless tracking. This land is mine. They don't know what to do with it. They cut down the trees and pave the tracks into roads and roar along the highways in their cars, all to pretend they know this place, that this wilderness is theirs.

But old Granny, she didn't have a clue. And when real wilderness came knocking, there was nothing she could do. We still have the old magics, all of us. We don't like to use it, we think it makes us a little more human. But if we really need to... well, we can stretch a bit of skin over a wolf's frame, and make the whole world think it's just another innocent Granny. Until one of us gets too smart, too greedy.

I shake my muzzle, a human movement, and get back on my way deep into the mountains they've dubbed the Rockies. Deep in my belly, hunger flexes its ugly claws.

I'm back to square one - no pack and no dinner. Just the last bits of Old Granny's skin sloughing off as I run.

Ruby and Romulus

By Kathleen Murphey

Once upon a time, there was a little girl named Ruby Red. She had flaming red hair and golden green eyes and was a joy to her family. Ruby grew up surrounded by women. Her grandmother and her great aunt lived on the other side of the great forest, and her mother, her Aunt Lauren, and her cousin, Cathy, lived in the small village by the river. The grands were healers and mid-wives, and they kept to themselves except when they were summoned to tend to someone who was ill or a woman in labor.

As Ruby grew up, she was sent to spend more and more time with the grands, so she could learn the ways of healing. They would show her pictures and samples of herbs, plants, flowers, barks, or mushrooms, and send her into the great forest to collect samples. They taught her how to treat the different items, which to mix together, which to make various teas, salves, poultices, and remedies, and so on.

At night in the cottage, the grands had Ruby read old myths and folk tales. They taught her to spin, knit, and sew. They had presented her with a basket and a sack with which to collect samples, an athame, a special dagger that healers used, and a bow and arrows to help her protect herself in the great forest. The athame also helped her collect samples. They regularly had her practice with the dagger and the bow. She got so good that she could supplement their goats' milk cheese, chicken eggs, cultivated and foraged fruits and vegetables, and occasional chicken dinners with hares, ducks, geese, fish, and other small game she hunted or snared in the great forest.

Most of the great forest was safe for Ruby to explore. Within the great forest, however, was a dense black woods that the grands warned Ruby never to enter. The black woods was a realm where the magical and the real world mixed, and strange things could happen there.

The grands explained that being a healer and midwife in their country in that time was a great honor, a great responsibility, and a great risk. "Men fear us, particularly church men, for we are women of power, and they don't like women to have power," they warned.

When Ruby's blood began to flow regularly, the grands also explained another unspoken fear that men had of women. They gave her a beautiful red velvet cloak that was lined with brown velvet, so the cloak was reversible. She could wear it with the red side underneath, hidden, like her sexuality, or she could wear it brazenly and with risk.

"Red is the color of life, of blood, and of passion. Men are hypocrites. They preach asexuality because what they fear most is female sexuality and passion, but what they really do is indulge or tolerate male sexuality and repress female sexuality. Look at the godly figures they hold up to the world: the Father, Son, and Holy Ghost, and the Virgin Mary. None of these is sexual unlike the ancient gods of the Greeks or the Romans or the Great Goddess religions. Do not fear your sexuality but be very careful with it. Some men would curse you for being sexual and perhaps even kill you, but you should know yourself as a sexual being even if that means only by self-exploration. Your blood flows now, child, and you will soon be capable of bearing children yourself. Men fear menstrual blood too because it is a part of women's ability to bear children that men do not possess. Red is the carnal color—of life, of passion, of blood, and of the flesh. Be carnal, but be careful with whom you share your carnal self."

Ruby loved her cloak and pondered the words of the grands. Their words frightened her, and she knew they were supposed to. She wondered, not for the first time, why it seemed so much more complicated and dangerous to be a girl. She had, of course, touched herself. She had heard the grands pleasing themselves in their beds in the small cottage, and she had heard her mother and her aunt do the same when she lived with them. It felt good. She didn't understand how something that felt so good could be considered so bad, but she had also seen how badly a girl was treated if she was unfortunate enough to get pregnant out of wedlock. The same consequences never applied to a boy. Mostly, she wore the cloak with the red side as lining. It was easier to move through the forest among the animals with the brown side showing. Some part of her also knew that she wore the red inside trying to grow comfortable with herself as a sexual being, not quite ready to wear it outwardly for all the world to see.

Time passed, and she blossomed into a young woman, sexually aware, but as yet, only sexually known to herself.

Ruby enjoyed the great forest. It felt like a sanctuary to her, a holy place full of stillness and quiet and yet teaming with life and noise—a place of life and death—like all the great mysteries of life—or at least that is what the grands said.

"Blood is a symbol of both life and death, and we find life and death in the great forest and in the river and in all places of great power. Respect the great forest for its bounty as well as for its dangers," they warned.

Sometimes the grands let Ruby take the pony into the great forest, and while she loved Gray Lady, she also liked how quietly she could walk through the great forest alone. One day Ruby was following a stream and collecting different mosses for the grands. She ventured further than usual into the great forest. She was humming contentedly to herself when she felt the small hairs on the back of neck stand up and goose bumps course over her skin. She whipped around scanning the great forest, but she could see nothing. Though she could see no animal or person, she felt eyes watching her. She drew her athame and backed away, retracing her steps until she felt comfortable enough to turn face-forward and hurry home.

She tried to explain that she felt like she was being watched to the grands, and they exchanged a worried look and admonished her to stick closer to the cottage for the next few days. Though she meant to stay close to the cottage the next day, she felt herself drawn deeper into the great forest until again she felt eyes watching her. But this time their presence did not alarm her so much. She felt them upon her, but the hairs did not stand up and the goose bumps didn't come. Slowly she turned, searching for the source of the gaze upon her, but she couldn't find it. She didn't run away this time, but lingered, more curious than afraid, but the eyes did not reveal themselves, and eventually, Ruby knew she had to get back and left, almost reluctantly.

When she next entered the great forest, she again felt drawn into its depths until she felt the presence of the eyes upon her. Again she couldn't locate their source, and frustrated now, she moved forward looking for them. And then they were gone; she felt their absence. They weren't looking at her. She froze in confusion. Had she scared their source? Why would they stop looking? What or who did they belong to? Then, as she stood there thinking, she felt them settle on her again but from further away. She realized that she liked the feel of the eyes upon her. She wanted to move forward again, but she didn't want to frighten them away again.

"Who are you? What are you?" she called softly, but there was no answer. Again she lingered, but nothing changed, so she moved forward again. As she passed a great oak tree she saw a small clearing and then the black woods came into view. She sensed that the gaze now came from the black woods, and she stopped, knowing that she shouldn't enter. "Come out," she said. "Show yourself to me, please," but her request was met with silence.

The next time Ruby went into the great forest she brought with her a lunch that could feed two with four apples and some goat cheese and a little bread. She sought out the black woods, and it didn't take long for her to feel the mysterious gaze settle on her. She walked toward it as far as she dared, and then she took off her cloak and spread in on the great forest floor with the brown side down and settled herself on the red cloth, taking off her weapons and laying them down next to her and taking out an apple. She bit into the apple and ate it slowly and quietly, straining her ears to see if she could hear anything moving toward her and combing the great forest for eyes or movement.

After a while, she suddenly caught sight of a pair of big glowing, golden yellow eyes looking at her through the trees. She couldn't see a face, but she saw strange eyes, bigger than animal eyes with a color that she didn't associate with human eyes. They stared at each other for a moment, and then the eyes closed and disappeared, but they reappeared in another spot. Again and again, they would appear, disappear, and reappear in a different spot, slowly getting closer.

"Who are you?" Ruby whispered.

And suddenly, a boy stepped out from behind a tree. Ruby sucked in her breathe, startled by the sudden revelation. Somehow the boy heard her change in breathing, and he froze, anxiety clouding his face, and she realized he was thinking of running away.

"Stay," she said softly. "You surprised me." She looked at him. His face relaxed slightly as he took in her words. He was a little older and taller than she was. He was muscular and darker skinned than she was. He had shoulder length brown wavy hair and golden yellow eyes that were staring at her with such intensity; she felt like they could almost burn her. He wore leather pants and a home spun shirt that was loosely laced across his chest. He was bare foot, and scattered stubble marked his cheeks. He was beautiful in a different, almost animalistic way.

"Who are you?" he asked back, in a voice that was deep and rough. "Why do you come here?"

"I come to get things for my grandmother and great aunt, herbs and mushrooms and things," she said trying to answer him.

"Girls don't usually enter the great forest alone," he said.

"Maybe I am not your typical girl. You've been watching me, why?" she replied.

He moved toward her cautiously. "I like the way you smell, and you're beautiful," he said softly, his face flushing with color. He squatted down just at the edge of her cloak, just feet from her.

"What is your name?" she asked, taking the opportunity to look at his eyes and his face more closely. His eyes were almost cat-like, glowing yellow gold, but his pupils were normal, human. His eye lashes were unusually long and thick for a boy's. He had full reddish/pink lips, and his nose was straight and short.

"I am Romulus," he answered hesitantly. He was still looking at her hungrily and warily at the same time, as if some part of him desperately wanted to be with her while another part told him he should run away and hide from her. "What is your name?"

Romulus, suckling of the She-wolf, Ruby thought to herself. "I am Ruby, Ruby Red. I brought some food," she said gesturing toward the sack in which she had the apples, cheese, and bread. "Would you like some?" she asked, patting a spot beside her on her cloak.

He looked at her with mingled horror and fascination. "You shouldn't be here," he said harshly, but he moved slightly closer to her.

She pulled out an apple and offered it to him, holding it in her hand. He moved closer, sitting himself on the very edge of her cloak. He started to move his hand toward her, but he seemed afraid to take the apple for some reason she didn't understand. She reached out and put the apple in his hand. As she did so, their hands touched, her finger tips brushing against his palm, and it was like an electric charge passed between them. He jerked his hand back, but she didn't move hers. It hadn't felt bad, just intense and different and full of something she couldn't describe. She stared at her hand and then at his hand.

"What was that?" she asked softly.

"I don't know," he said, blushing again. The apple was still in his hand, and after he recovered himself a little, he ate it, more like devoured it, in what seemed like three bites. "It is good. What is it?"

"It's an apple," she answered incredulously. "Haven't you ever had an apple before?"

"No," he hesitated. He was holding something back yet wanting to reveal it too. "There aren't any where I am from."

Here she sensed was the source of his unease, the conflict that made him want to be there and yet told him to run. "And where are you from that there are no apples?" she asked.

"I live in the black woods," he whispered so quietly that it was hard to hear him, and she almost wasn't sure she had heard him correctly.

"The black woods?" she repeated in a whisper to match his own. She looked up to find him scrutinizing her face with brutal intensity, searching for signs of recognition or revulsion or fear, but she returned his gaze evenly and calmly. She knew what he had to be. He was a werewolf in his human form, a werewolf boy who was attracted to a human girl, and he was beautiful and here with her, risking himself to be with her. She knew how the villagers would react to meeting one of his kind.

"How long have you been following me?" she asked.

Again his eyes searched her face demandingly as he tried to read her reactions to his answers. "I didn't mean to at first. I began to recognize your scent when you were in the great forest, even from the black woods, and I was drawn to it, but I would stay out of range and just watch you from afar or listen to you. I like your singing and humming. You have a pretty voice. Maybe a few weeks like that. You're not like other human girls, and then I wondered just how different you were."

Nothing he said alarmed her, so she continued to look at him calmly. She had been drawn to him as well. She was drawn to him now. She wanted to see what would happened if they touched again. She moved a little closer to him, but she stopped as she felt his body go rigid in alarm. "What do you mean 'just how different I was'?" she asked him.

"You're so beautiful, Ruby," and she was shocked at how pleased she was to hear him say her name. "So bold wandering the great forest. I … I … wondered … if you would be … bold enough … to talk to me," and his voice was quiet again, barely audible. His face flushed as he said the words. She reached her hand toward his, and he tensed but didn't move away. Slowly, he moved his hand back toward hers, and then very gently, he placed his hand over hers and her skin burned and tingled where he touched her. Her breath caught, but so did his. They stared at each other, watching and waiting and feeling. Sensation seemed to move across their skin surprising them with the intensity. He moved closer.

"Is that why you came closer four days ago?" she asked breathlessly.

"Yes," he breathed. "I shouldn't have crossed out of the black woods, and you shouldn't want to see me, but I want you to want to see me, and impossibly, you are here." They were very close now, and they both knew they were about to kiss. His face bent toward hers, and she inclined her face up to his. Their lips brushed against each other teasingly, full of anticipatory longing, and the burning sensation was there too, tingling with a rush of desire, and then the kiss started for real, his lips parting hers, his tongue probing hers, his hands knotting into her hair, and she was kissing him back and winding her arms around his neck. The intensity of the kiss grew. Everywhere they touched burned with sensation, and perhaps it was so much that they forgot to breath because they had to pull away from each other panting, trying to catch their breathes.

He was laughing, and she realized she was too, with relief and happiness. She had found a boy who she liked, and though he was a werewolf that didn't seem to be a barrier that had to separate them, and he had found a girl who he liked, and though she was a human girl that didn't seem to be a barrier to separate them either. They talked softly, asking each other about everything and eating the food that she had brought. He had never had cheese or bread before either. Mostly he ate meat, fish, grasses, berries, herbs, and some wild varieties of vegetables. She told him about the grands and what she was learning from them. His pack was small, nine or so werewolves, mostly bonded pairs, but two were only cubs and then himself. He didn't know how much trouble he would be in when he returned. He could try to bathe in a stream before going back, but they would still smell her on him. She knew she would need to tell the grands, and she had absolutely no idea how they would take the news. They weren't like the villagers with their irrational prejudices, but they had warned her not to enter the black woods and she knew that would also mean not cavorting with beings who lived there.

She realized it was getting late and that she needed to go so that she would return home safely before nightfall. He realized it too, and he pulled her into his lap for another kiss. They were touching in more places than ever before, their bodies pressed together, and everywhere burned and tingled. The blood surged through their veins, and she could feel their hunger for each other. She wanted him to touch her more, in the places that she had only explored by herself, and she could tell that he wanted her to touch him in his private places too, but they contented themselves with the kiss, letting it flame with intensity until she was wrapped around him and he was pressing her closer to his body. Finally, she pulled away panting and disengaged herself from his body. He let her go reluctantly, and they stood up and moved off her cloak. He bent to retrieve it for her, shaking off the great forest floor debris and placing it around her shoulders. She retrieved the sack and her weapons, and they said good-bye with a fleeting kiss and a promise to see each other the next day.

The grands could tell Ruby was agitated, and they wanted to know what was going on. She told them she had met a boy in the woods and that she liked him. When she told them his name, they knew immediately that he was the one who had been watching her and that he was a werewolf. They were filled with a mix of emotions.

"You have managed to engage yourself with one of the few beings that the village men and especially the church fathers would find more offensive than a sexually active girl. You do realize that?" they demanded. They huffed and puffed. They didn't like it, but they wouldn't forbid her from seeing him. A condition they mandated was meeting him which she thought was only fair. She would have to talk to Romulus about it. She wondered what he would think of that. She wondered how he was faring in the black woods.

Romulus bathed in the stream, rolling over and over and scrubbing his skin uncomfortably against the rocks, but he knew it would not be enough. He entered the black woods and made his way cautiously to the pack. As he neared, he heard the growling as they picked up Ruby's scent on him.

"Have you killed a human?" demanded the angry voice of the alpha male.

"No," Romulus started to answer.

"No," cut in the elder male. "He has touched one and been touched by one."

"Are you insane?" asked the alpha male. "It is too dangerous. It is not done!"

Romulus cowered before the alpha male. "She is the grand-daughter of the healers. She is not of the village," he said in his defense. "She is different."

"Grand-daughter of the healers? The Red women?" the elder male said questioningly. "Clan leader, there could be advantages in this to us."

"Perhaps," conceded the alpha male, "but there is risk too."

"There is always risk," the elder male answered calmly.

The alpha male beckoned to Romulus, "Explain yourself."

"I like her. I like her a lot...I...I love her," he choked out.

The alpha male stared at him, caught off guard by the depth of boy's feelings. "And she is not afraid of you—repulsed by you?" he asked skeptically.

"Apparently not," Romulus answered blushing furiously.

"She reciprocates your feelings, your desire?" he asked incredulously.

Romulus hesitated. "I kissed her, and she kissed me," he said very quietly, and he heard the collective gasps as the whole pack digested this information.

"We will consider this matter," said the alpha male.

Romulus retreated and watched warily as the alpha and his mate consulted with the elders.

The next day, Ruby entered the great forest eagerly. Romulus found her easily, catching her in his arms and holding her closely. The shock of their touch rocked them both, and they kissed and pulled apart before they could be overcome.

"The grands want to meet you," she said breathlessly.

"The alpha, his mate, and elders want to meet you and them too," he answered.

"Really?" she asked.

"Really," he answered. "Perhaps tomorrow. Could the grands make it to the northern stream where it forks at noon?"

Ruby considered this. They could ride and tether the horse and pony a safe distance away and walk to the fork. "Yes. They would ride most of the way. We could tether the horse and pony far enough away, so the animals wouldn't be spooked by your scents, and we could walk the rest of the distance to the meeting point."

Ruby set down her basket and took off her weapons, and Romulus pulled Ruby back into his arms. She looked up at him with shining eyes; they stood there a moment, memorizing the features of their faces until Romulus reached up to pull back the hood of her cloak and free her hair, running his fingers through it and letting it to spill down her shoulders and back. "I missed you," he said softly.

"As I missed you," she answered back. He pressed his lips to hers, gently, and they could feel the intensity of their touching, even through their clothes. His hands reached to undo her cloak, and when they fumbled, her hands met his and pulled the tie free. Gently he pulled the cloak from her shoulders and spread it on the great forest floor as she had done the day before to make a circular blanket for them.

Self-consciously they moved to the center of the cloak and seated themselves next to each other. He reached up to cup her face in his hands, and then he was scooting closer to her and inclining her face towards his and bending his to hers. Her lips trembled against his, spiking a wave of desire in him, and he greedily parted her lips and kissed her. Her arms wound around his neck, and the feel of her fingers running through his hair made him growl softly in the back of his throat. The sound and soft vibration made her crazy with desire, and she found herself climbing onto his lap, straddling him with her legs, her skirts settling around them. She kissed him fiercely, and their bodies felt like they could burst into flame.

Finally, the kissing and the touching through clothes was not enough, and Ruby reached for his shirt, and he helped her pull it over his shoulders and head in a smooth motion, casting it aside. Her hands combed over his chest, and everywhere she touched burned. Her fingers traced over the muscles of his chest, and she played with the hair there at the same time as her mouth moved to his neck. The kisses changed to sucking and gentle biting. He groaned with pleasure, feeling that he could completely dissolve in her arms. Then he wanted to touch her too, to feel her naked skin against him, but her clothing was so much more complicated than his. He reached for her bodice, and she pulled away slightly so that she could help him unlace it and show him how. With it unlaced, they pulled it and her blouse off and cast them aside. He stared at the soft, pale flesh of her naked chest for a moment, and marveled at the fullness of her small, rounded breasts, so different from his own.

She was so beautiful, even more beautiful than he could have imagined. Her shapely breasts aroused him painfully, and the hungry way he looked at her made her blush. He pulled her against him, so that their bare chests pressed against each other and their skin burned and their blood raced. He move his mouth down her neck mauling her throat as his hands caressed her breasts until she moaned in pleasure, and he pulled away from her because if they didn't stop, they would continue until they were naked and mated. They stared at each other, panting and trying to calm and steady themselves.

"I never knew I could feel like this," he whispered.

She nodded in agreement, "So totally overcome," she added.

"Yes." He reached for her blouse and helped her dress, enjoying lacing her into her bodice. He put on his shirt reluctantly. They got up, and he retrieved her cloak for her, shaking it off and draping it around her shoulders. She armed herself and took up the basket. He asked her to show him some of the things she collected for the grands, so they walked through the great forest pausing as Ruby took samples of this or that. She paused at one point. She was so curious but she wasn't sure how to ask.

He looked at her searchingly. "What is it, Ruby?" he asked.

"I just wondered… what… you," she began but blushed before she could finish.

But he guessed easily, "What I look like as a wolf?"

"Yes," she breathed.

"Are you sure you want to see me like that?" he asked and his voice was conflicted, afraid that he would scare her, and yet also hopeful, that his beastly form wouldn't.

Understanding his hesitation and desperate to show him her devotion, she answered him firmly, "Yes, I want to see you, every way that you are."

Carefully, he stepped away from her, and he fell to his knees and then rose up, four legged and furry with a tail, and his face elongated, his nose and mouth becoming a muzzle and his teeth transforming into canine teeth. His eyes remained the same, glowing golden yellow, and his hair was the same brown, with the hair around his chest and neck thicker and longer than the rest. He was magnificent, strong and lean. Her breath caught as she looked at him, and she could see the anxiety in his eyes, but she moved close to him and ran her fingers through his hair and bent only slightly to kiss his forehead. He growled that same low growl of pleasure in the back of his throat that he had done earlier but it sounded different, louder and lusher, in his wolf form. He stepped back from her and barked, a happy bark of relief, and then he changed back into himself or at least the human boy she knew.

He moved toward her catching her in his arms. "You're really okay?" he asked, unsure but hopeful.

"You're just as beautiful and impressive as a wolf as you are as a boy," she said looking deeply into his eyes, and she saw him fight back the sudden tears that welled in them. She touched his cheek and brushed her lips across his.

"You are everything to me," he whispered, and then he kissed her until they had to break apart from each other panting. Then it was time for Ruby to return home, and they parted.

The grands agreed to the meeting, explaining that a relationship between Ruby and Romulus would be a special kind of alliance, filled with both risk and opportunity. They grilled her on her feelings toward Romulus. She explained about their powerful physical attraction to each other, not without blushing furiously. They nodded and told her that they thought, though Ruby would be associating herself with werewolves, that she could be fully sexual with him without danger, unlike with a boy from the village. They talked to her about the ways that women and men could be intimate. They explained that it could hurt her a little the first time. They warned her that wolves mate for life and asked if she was willing to take on that responsibility and commitment. They warned her that she might have to become a werewolf herself, and they told her about her great-great grandmother, Little Red Riding Hood, who had married a werewolf and had been found out by the villagers and eventually had to change into a werewolf to escape them. The villagers had changed the story, of course, but the real story was that Little Red had been happy with her wolf and he with her. They didn't press her for answers, but asked her to think on things during the night and to try to have some answers in the morning.

Ruby thought fitfully over the all the grands had brought to her attention. What did she feel for Romulus? Was she the one for him? Was he the one for her? What would the black woods be like? What magical things would she be able to see and find? What would it be like living with a pack of werewolves? What if she became a werewolf herself? It was overwhelming. She didn't know what to think. She tried to calm herself.

Did she love him? Could she love him? She felt for him powerfully. She knew in her heart that he was a better match for her than any boy in the village. Yes, she decided, she could commit to him. The black woods? What scared her the most was how she would be received by Romulus' pack, but perhaps she would feel better after meeting with the alphas and elders.

In the morning, Ruby told the grands how she felt. She did her chores around the cottage and farm: feeding the chickens, gathering eggs, milking the goats, setting the milk for cheese, and tending their kitchen garden. Soon it was time for them to travel, and she saddled Blaze for the grands, who rode together, and Gray Lady for herself. They rode as close to the meeting place as they felt was safe and tethered the horse and pony, and then walked the distance to the fork in the stream.

The alpha male was a powerfully built man with flowing golden brown hair and dark blue eyes. His mate was blonder and slighter, feminine, but imposing. She had yellow gold eyes similar to Romulus'. The elder male had salt and pepper gray hair with glowing green eyes; his body was muscular and imposing but obviously diminished from his former glory. His mate was brown haired with streaks of gray and wide gray eyes. They wore simple clothing. The men in leather pants and home spun shirts and the women home spun frocks belted at the waists. Romulus stood with them, his face baring the emotions that he felt: anxiety, happiness, relief, and longing—all at the same time.

Little Red and her wolf were the precedent for the relationship between Ruby and Romulus, both sides acknowledged that. That Ruby was not a village girl, a healer/mid-wife in training, and the grand-daughter and grand-niece of two very capable healer/mid-wives were all to her favor. Ruby would not draw as much attention to herself since she wasn't of the village. Further, she could use her training on the pack members, and in cases that were beyond her care, she could get the assistance of the grands. To Romulus' favor was his devotion to Ruby and his and the pack's ability to protect her in the black woods. What was also in his favor but left unsaid was his werewolf appreciation of Ruby's sexuality instead of the typical human male fear of it and hostility toward it. Ruby would be able to spend time there in the black woods with the pack and with Romulus, but she would also be able to gather things, magical things that were unavailable elsewhere, and bring them to the grands. It was acknowledged that in the course of their relationship it might be necessary to turn Ruby into a werewolf for her own protection. Both sides understood the risks, and yet both sides could see and feel the obvious delight that Ruby and Romulus took from each other's company. Consent was given. Ruby walked the grands back to Blaze and Gray Lady, and the two older women rode Blaze home with Gray Lady trailing behind them. The alpha, his mate, and the elders disappeared into the great forest, and Ruby and Romulus were left alone.

They walked for a while until they found a spot they liked and then they spread out Ruby's cloak on the great forest floor. Soon they were kissing and touching with a frenzied excitement. His shirt came off and then her bodice and blouse, and then that wasn't enough and more clothing was shed. He touched her all over and then between her legs until she cried out in pleasure. She touched him too, but when she reached for him, but he stopped her.

"If I come too, they will think we have mated. They will be able to smell you on me in this new way as well as just the scent of your skin and hair. If I come too, they will smell that and assume," he explained.

She looked at him, and she could tell that it was painful for him to stop, not just physically but emotionally too. He wanted to go further so badly, but he was trying to protect her, and she realized that she didn't care what they thought. She wanted to go farther too. If they thought they were mated if he came, then why not mate? "Then, let's mate," she whispered, color flooding her face.

"Ruby?" he said, his golden eyes searching her face.

"Don't stop touching me, Romulus," she implored him.

He growled softly, and the rest of their clothes were off, and he entered her gently at first and then more forcefully. He came quickly, and she had brought some spare rags for the fluid that the grands told her would be the result of the sexual union of a girl and a boy. They lay together in each other's arms, a little stunned at what they had done.

After a while, he propped himself up to look down at her, and she laughed thinking of the village story.

"My, what big eyes you have," she teased.

His eyes danced with amusement. "The better to leer lustfully at you, Ruby Red," he answered playfully.

"My, what big ears you have," she continued.

"The better to hear you moan with pleasure, my love."

She flushed and added, "My, what big hands you have."

"The better to touch every inch of your body with, my darling," and he traced his hand over her breast and down to her hip.

"My, what a big mouth you have."

"The better to kiss you with and lick you with and suck you with, my sweet," his lips turning up in a grin.

"My, what big teeth you have," she said, finishing her parody of the village tale.

"The better to bite you with," and he put his mouth to her throat and mauled her neck until she was panting and running her fingers through his hair.

"You know that wolves mate for life," he said cautiously, his heart racing in his chest, his lips just below her ear.

"Yes," she answered softly.

"Marry me?" he whispered, afraid to look at her, afraid she would say no.

"Yes," she said. She had already decided it would be him, both last night after talking with the grands and in the decision to mate with him. "I love you," she added, saying the words out loud for the first time and knowing that they were true for her, and she pulled away a little so that she could see his face.

He laughed with relief, "Really?"

"Yes, really, Romulus. Will it make it easier for you, us getting married?" she asked.

"I am not sure," he answered slowly. "They know I love you, but that we have mated…so quickly…well…I think that will surprise them. It sort of surprises me," color flushing his face. "Will the grands know? Will they be surprised?"

She reached out to touch his face, "I don't know if they will know, but they have made it clear to me that my sexuality is mine to explore and do what I want with. Their main concern is that my partner loves me."

"I do love you, Ruby," and he took one of her hands in his and brought it to his lips so that he could kiss it. "I have loved you since the first time I really saw you with your green gold eyes and flaming red hair and the way you smelled of lavender soap and human girl." He paused, "You know it won't be an official human marriage, don't you?"

"What, no village riot at the reception lead by the church fathers themselves?" she teased.

He smiled slightly, "It is funny, but it's not, and the not funny part is that it could all be too true—we could become the hunted. Ruby, are you sure this is what you want—a life with me?" and there was pain in his voice and in the look in his eyes.

She looked at him, her hand tracing down his cheek around his jaw under his chin and up the other jaw and cheek. His eyes closed to savor the sensation of her touch. "I know it hasn't been very long, but we are past the point of going back. We're mated and engaged. How soon do you think we can be married?" she asked.

"Whenever the grands agree to it," he answered, relief clear in his voice, and he leaned over her bending down to kiss her gently, tenderly. They dressed quietly, each lost in thoughts about how their lives had so completely changed in the last few days and how much more they would change again once they were married.

Romulus again tried to wash the scents of Ruby from his body in the stream. His return to the pack wasn't met with growling but with blatant stares of disbelief. The alpha male glanced in the direction of the deeper black woods, and Romulus jogged to his side and followed him through the trees.

When they were some distance away, the alpha slowed his pace, "You've mated with her?" he asked. "Already?" the shock and disapproval clear in his voice.

"Yes," Romulus answered quietly. "I told you that I loved her. She loves me too. We couldn't stop. She said that she would marry me."

"Couldn't or wouldn't stop," the alpha said harshly. "You could offend the Red women. They could go to the villagers," he paused. "Marry? She understands about our bonding?"

"Ruby doesn't think her grandmother or great aunt will be offended. Yes, she understands about our bonding."

They heard the approach of the elder male and waited for him to join them. "You rash pup, what were you thinking?" chided the elder, but a smiled played at the edges of his mouth.

"He wasn't thinking. That's exactly the problem. It's too impossibly sudden, too reckless, too intense," said the alpha.

"I can't explain it. She's all I can think about." Romulus struggled to explain, "I noticed her weeks ago. I could smell her from the black woods. I had to be around her, and then she was willing to see me a few days ago. When we touch, it's like fire," he said blushing furiously. "Sometimes I feel like we could burst into flame. I know it is too intense, but I don't know how to make it less so. She drives me wild."

"That is how the attraction between Lucian and Little Red has always been described when I have heard about it," answered the elder, "as a love almost like madness. That's why I came, Alpha. I thought you might want to know that before judging the boy too harshly." He turned then, returning to the pack and leaving them alone.

"Romulus, we will wait to see what the Red women say of this new development. I hope it will be received as you say, for all our sakes," and they returned to the pack.

Ruby returned to the cottage. She was subdued but happy, not sure exactly how to present Romulus' proposal to the grands and equally unsure about how they would react. They watched her carefully at dinner as she toyed with her food and was unusually quiet, but they didn't press her about it until after dinner when the dishes were cleared, washed, and put away.

"Out with it, child. What happened today with you and Romulus? What is it that you need to tell us?"

She paused and looked at them cautiously, "He asked me… to… marry him," she said very quietly.

"Marry him?" they stammered, exchanging alarmed glances and looking back at her. "It's been three days, child," and they watched the color flood Ruby's cheeks. She heard them gasp in unison, and though she couldn't imagine her face getting even redder, she felt like it had.

"You've mated, haven't you?" and though there was accusation in their tones, there was also an amusement and even a little admiration for her boldness. They clucked at her and at each other. "You'll need to tell your mother. You'll need to visit the village. Hopefully, it goes without saying that you will tell her and only her. A wedding. A great forest wedding at sunset and then under the stars," they gushed. "A great grandbaby in less than a year! There are herbs and teas you must start taking, my dear."

Early the next day, the grands helped Ruby saddle Gray Lady, and after they loaded her up with herbs and salves and gifts for her mother, aunt, and cousin, they waved her off. She was highly uncomfortable leaving with Romulus unaware of where she was and what she was doing. She wondered if he would find her in the great forest before she got very close to the village. If he didn't find her, she thought she might cry. However, she also knew she had to see her mother and the sooner the better.

Just as she was afraid that she had gone beyond where he would dare to go, she heard Romulus call her name from a distance, giving her a chance to tether the pony and walk to him. Anxiety lined his face, and it pained her that she was the source of his discomfort.

"Where are you going?" he asked.

"The grands told me that I needed to tell my mother, about us, about the wedding," she said, and she saw to her horror that this explanation did not relieve him but drove up his level of distress. She realized he was drawing the most negative conclusion possible. "No, not like that. She is my mother. She needs to know; no one in the village will know."

He didn't seem particularly assured, but he pulled her into his arms, pulling the hood of her cloak down and nuzzling his face in her hair, and then they were greedily kissing and touching each other, and when they broke apart, he led her to a small stand of trees, and they spread out the cloak, so they could be together once more, kissing, licking, touching, sucking and gently biting, moaning in pleasure, making her come, and then mating. They had been too frantic to do much more than murmur each other names and profess their love, but as they cleaned up and dressed, they told each other what had happened when they faced their families. She was interested in what the elder male had said about the love between Little Red and Lucian, and he was intensely relieved to hear how the grands had taken the wedding news. He didn't like the idea of her being in the village at all. She would spend the night in her mother's house and leave again in the morning. She promised to see him the next afternoon, and he reluctantly let her go, kissing her in parting.

She rode again, and as she neared the village, she noticed some people in the great forest. Several wood cutters labored, and a few boys were hunting, with no particular success. A group of children gathered sticks under the supervision of one of the wood cutter's wives, but Romulus appeared to be right. Girls didn't enter the great forest alone, and almost no one traveled so far alone in the great forest as did she and the grands, but she wondered if the grands counted the same way because they normally traveled together.

Her mother was pleased to see her and pulled her into a tight embrace. They put the Gray Lady in the barn and got her oats and water and took off her saddle and tack. They caught up on household news, and though her mother knew Ruby had come for a specific purpose, she waited for Ruby to tell her in own time and in her own way. Aunt Lauren and Cathy seemed almost as pleased to see her as her mother. After Ruby had had some tea and cheese and fruit, Ruby asked to see her mother alone, and they retreated to her mother's bedroom, and Ruby told her mother everything—about feeling watched in the great woods, about meeting Romulus, about how intensely they seemed feel for each other, and about their mating and his asking to marry her. Ruby's mother listened to her daughter intensely, studying the features of her face as she spoke.

"And you want this, Ruby? You want to marry this werewolf boy when you are so young? When it will put you both at risk? Put even your families at risk?" she asked her voice full of concern and wariness.

"I do, Mother. He is all that I think about. I mean I can think about other things, but he is always also on my mind. I feel like I need him, being so far away from him now is painful, and this morning when I thought I wouldn't see him for two days, I was utterly miserable."

"When?"

"The grands were thinking next Saturday night."

Her mother looked at her for a long moment. "All right," she said at last. "But I want to make you a gift. Come with me." Her mother led Ruby out of the house and down the street to her uncle's smithy. He was wrapping up his work at the forge, but he looked up as they entered, and he smiled warmly at his sister and Ruby. Ruby's mother explained that she wanted a set of copper rings, one for Ruby and one for a boy. Uncle William seemed to take note of the vagueness of her mother's references to a boy, but he said nothing.

He took Ruby's hand and wrapped a piece of string around one finger, cutting the string so that the ends just met. Then Uncle William held out his own hand and asked Ruby to estimate which of his fingers was closest to the index finger of the boy in question. Uncle William was a full grown man and a smith. His fingers were thick and calloused. If Ruby had to guess, she thought his pinky was the closest. Her uncle saw her hesitation and called for his oldest son, Will, who was eighteen. Will presented his hands to Ruby. She blushed as she did it, but she took one of Will's hands in one of her own and interlaced their fingers together. Yes, she thought Will's hands were of a similar size to Romulus', so her uncle cut another piece of string to fit around one of Will's fingers.

Her mother pulled her brother to the side and spoke to him softly, and then she left with Ruby. She said nothing until they were back at the house. Wedding rings were normally made of silver or gold, she explained. Gold was too expensive for her to afford, and silver wouldn't due for a werewolf. Copper would work, but William would suspect the reason which would be confirmed when Ruby didn't get married in the village. She had told her brother. Seeing the alarm run over Ruby's face, her mother assured her that William wouldn't tell a soul. The Red family knew its history even if the rest of the village had fabricated its own version of that history, her mother explained.

They ate a pleasant meal with Aunt Lauren and Cathy. Ruby brought out the various supplies and gifts that the grands had sent to her mother, aunt, and cousin. They swapped more news and stories, and then Ruby went up to bed with Cathy. She fell asleep thinking about her reunion with Romulus.

Romulus had bathed on his way back to the black woods. His return was not remarked on, but as the day wore on, his anxiety and agitation were noticeable. The elder male approached him, "What is it, my boy? Walk with me and tell me," he requested. When they were out of ear shot of the rest of the pack, Romulus told him that Ruby was going to the village to tell her mother of the wedding. At first, the elder was as alarmed as Romulus had been, but then Romulus had explained all that Ruby had told him including the grands' suggestion of the following Saturday night for the wedding.

"So this agitation, this restless energy, is from being separated from her?" the elder asked wonderingly.

"Yes, I guess—that and her being in the village—even for a good reason," Romulus answered, perhaps a little too sharply.

The elder raised his eyebrows. "You have it bad, Romulus."

"I know," he admitted. "What will happen once we are married? Where will we live? How can we be together without the whole pack listening?" he asked miserably. Though the pack members lived in small cottages grouped together, pairs did their mating in the black woods in places where they knew they could be alone. Romulus wasn't sure he could take Ruby that far into the black woods, which was why he had risked the places in the great forest that were closest to the black woods—places that were far away from both humans and werewolves.

"There is Little Red and Lucian's cottage not all that far from here. It hasn't been used since then, and the disuse has made it largely hidden, but it could be cleaned up for you," the elder said pensively.

"Could we go there? Would you show it to me?" he asked pleadingly.

"Not tonight. But I will take you tomorrow. It will give you something to do while you wait her return," and the elder smiled at Romulus.

"What about during the full moon?" Romulus asked hesitantly.

"It was my understanding that the cottage was enchanted somehow—that Little Red could not be harmed there even during the full moon, but Ruby has an additional option. She has her grandmother and great aunt. It might be nice for her to spend those nights with them, so she does not completely lose her human family," the elder said thoughtfully.

With Romulus comforted, they returned to the pack.

In the morning, Ruby was surprised that her mother and her aunt had combed through their belongings looking for fine clothing. They had come up with a beautiful linen blouse that was trimmed in lace, a midnight blue velvet bodice and a matching long fitted shirt. There were several other plainer linen shirts and a brown leather bodice and a burgundy brocade bodice. They presented these items to her in the morning and packed them in her bags. Her mother would make the trip for the wedding, and they all said a teary good-bye. Despite the sorrow she felt at leaving her family, Ruby also felt a sense of relief at being able to leave and return to the grands, the great forest, and Romulus, so the ride was pleasant.

Romulus was up early, but he forced himself to stay calm and contain his energy. The elder male would take him, so he couldn't afford to annoy the man before he was ready to go. The elder seemed to sense Romulus distress and hurried. They ran part way to burn off some of Romulus' energy, and then they came to a densely wooded area. In fact, it seemed almost impassible between the denseness of the trees and the debris that littered the spaces in between. By squeezing through the trees and pushing debris out of the way, they got through about ten feet. Suddenly, the density ended, and a clearing rose before them in the center of which was a little cottage. It had only two rooms: a kitchen area with a hearth and stove and work surfaces and a small bedroom. It was dirty and dusty. The roof was in disarray, and the shutters weren't hanging straight. But it was miraculous to Romulus. He could clean it and fix things before Saturday, and he and Ruby could be in the black woods alone, not with the pack all the time.

Romulus looked at the elder, and he flushed to see that the man had been looking at him for some time with a bemused look on his face. "Thank you," Romulus choked out, and the older man smiled and said, "I'll leave you to it then," and left Romulus alone with his project. Romulus found a bucket and went outside, there was a small stream not far from the house, so he filled the bucket and went back to the cottage wiping down surfaces until the water needed to be changed, and he spent the morning cleaning and passing the time.

At mid-afternoon, when it seemed possible for Ruby to be home, Romulus left the cottage and headed toward the great forest. Ruby had gotten home, and having attended to Gray Lady in the stable and relating the most pressing news to the grands, she went looking for Romulus. He heard her and smelled her before she knew he was there. The relief he felt in seeing that she was all right and had returned to him from the village, felt as if a physical weight had been lifted from his shoulders. He ran to her, catching her in his arms and spinning her around.

She laughed at the enthusiasm of his embrace, but she was pleased too. It had filled her with anxiety when he hadn't met her in the great forest during her return.

He pulled down her hood and pulled her hair free running his fingers through it as he did so. He bent to kiss her, and though he tried to tame it, he could stop the urgency of the kiss, of his physical need for her, and she wound her arms around him in response, kissing him back with a kindred passion. Finally, they pulled apart gasping, and he undid her cloak and spread it hastily on the great forest floor. He pulled her down on the cloak where he unashamedly started liberating her from her clothing. Soon they were both naked and kissing, touching, licking sucking, biting, and pleasuring each other, moaning and murmuring as they went. After he made her come, he came quickly, and they lay together in each other's arms for a few moments before pulling apart and cleaning themselves.

Sated physically, they began to catch up with each other. She took his hand and looked at it closely, confirming that his fingers were much like those of Will's. She explained that her mother wanted them to have rings for the wedding, and he was charmed by the idea of a copper wedding ring. She told him that her mother intended to come to the wedding, and he told her about the cottage that had belonged to Little Red and Lucian. They parted reluctantly agreeing when and where to meet the following day.

And so it went for the days up until Saturday with Romulus spending time at the cottage cleaning it, fixing things, the roof and the shutters, finding fresh pine needles for the mattress and restuffing it, finding sweet smelling herbs to hang in the kitchen and the bedroom. He still found time to spend with Ruby, mating with her and talking to her. Ruby enjoyed her time with Romulus but was commandeered into all sorts of wedding preparations, which largely meant food preparation. Extra cheeses were made; fruit was collected from their trees and gardens but also from the great forest. In the two days before the wedding lots of bread was made. Ruby's mother arrived the Friday afternoon before the wedding bringing her own stores of butter and jams and throwing herself into the food preparation.

That Saturday at late afternoon, the grands had attached a flatbed cart full of food to Blaze's saddle and had ridden close to the fork in the northern stream. They unhitched the cart at the closest point they thought Blaze could stand and then moved him safely away. The alpha's mate and the elder female met the grands. They were supervising spits of venison and wild pig, and the four women moved the food from the cart to tables that had been constructed and lined the area where the wedding would take place.

The four women realized they respected each other—both sides had made an effort to make this a special event. The werewolves realized the care the human women had taken to provide them food they couldn't get in the black woods. They asked about each other carefully, gleaning information. Both sides found that they shared much including the love of their children and the child they suspected was growing or would be growing in Ruby's womb.

Ruby's mother had helped Ruby dress in the fine white linen shirt with the lace trim and the midnight blue velvet bodice and skirt. She had brushed Ruby's hair, then woven an array of pretty white flowers in a cascade of braids and curls that framed Ruby's face elegantly. As they were leaving the cottage, Ruby moved to put on her cloak in her usual manner, but her mother took it from her and reversed the linings so that the red side showed and the brown was hidden. Her mother's gesture made Ruby blush. It was time for Ruby to acknowledge herself as a fully sexual female with the carnal color wrapped around her like a mantle instead of hidden. With the sun flashing its fading golden light, Ruby, in her cloak, glowed like fire moving through the great forest or at least that is how she looked to Romulus as he watched her approach, a flaming light to give meaning to his life. He could only hope he could provide her with as much inspiration and comfort.

Rough logs had been placed on either side of a narrow path so that the werewolves and their few human guests could sit while Ruby and Romulus said their vows publically. Most of the pack members had been milling around, but they began to take their seats when they saw that Ruby had arrived. Ruby and her mother were met by the grands and the alpha and elder couples and Romulus. Over the past two days, this group had met several times to meet and get to know each other better. The elder couple and the grands seemed to find the situation inevitable and even romantic, but perhaps that was because they had heard the genesis of the current story from people who actually seen and witnessed the love between Little Red and Lucian. Ruby's mother and the alpha couple were less enthusiastic but accepting. After speaking briefly, they dispersed to take their seats leaving Ruby with Romulus.

Romulus pulled Ruby toward him and kissed her forehead. "I like the red," he whispered huskily. Then he untied the cloak and pulled it from her head and shoulders, setting it aside so that he could look at her. "You look so beautiful," he said softly. His normal attire had been replaced by a slightly finer set of leather pants, shirt, and leather jacket. He took her hand, and they walked together to stand before their families. The ceremony was simple, but cast against a magnificent blazing sunset, it made the scene almost magical. Ruby and Romulus said their vows and exchanged the rings that Ruby's mother had given them. After the words were said, they kissed, and then there were embraces and introductions. Ruby was introduced to the pack members she had not yet met, as were her mother and the grands. Torches were set, and the food and the company were pleasant.

When everyone had eaten his or her full, the company broke up. Ruby's mother and the grands were given torches to light their way back to Blaze and then to the cottage, and the werewolves disappeared into the night. Romulus wrapped Ruby in her cloak, and her hand in his, he led her through the forest and into the black woods to the cottage that had been Little Red's and Lucian's and would now be theirs.

Someone had lit a merry little fire in the hearth. Romulus suspected the elder male, so there was soft light in the cottage when Romulus carried his bride over the threshold. He set her down so she could look around. She was charmed by the little cottage, and almost forgot herself in thinking about their shared future life there until she felt his hands at the tie of her cloak, undoing it and pulling it from her head and shoulders. He cast it aside and pulled her up into his arms again and carried her into their bedroom. Somehow he managed to rip the top sheet and blanket down and place her gently on the bed.

They scrambled out of their clothes, and though they had never minded mating in great forest, there was something wonderful about being alone in a proper bed in a bedroom, and even more wonderful still was the knowledge that they didn't need to be parted. They didn't need to separate to go home because they were home. Basking in that sweet knowledge, their kisses and caresses began slowly, tenderly. Her hands exploring his body, and his hands exploring hers. The kissing, touching, licking, sucking, biting, and pleasuring each other continued until they had both come, and after they had wiped themselves off, they snuggled into each other's arms, savoring the contact between their naked skin and whispering to each other until they fell asleep—not as innocent characters in a fairy tale but as fully aware sexual partners.

Inspired By

Aladdin and His

Magic Carpet

The Carpet

By Matthew Wilson

Stan Tallard had always been compulsive. That's why he'd inadvertently burned half his face off on his stag night trying to out-do the fire-eater and spit mouthfuls of gin onto his lighter.

And that's why he bought the magic carpet. A deal with which he was quite pleased with, until Alice threw the frying pan in his direction. Of course he understood they were hard up and that Stan was facing the sack at work. People were put off by his scars as surely as Alice had lost her love for him that same awful night, but to show she wasn't shallow, she'd gone through with the tense ceremony. She couldn't face going back on her word when she'd invited her family from overseas.

But this was a MAGIC CARPET. The eBay advert had said so. It would be crazy not to have bought it.

"Honey, £1500 is a steal. D'you know how much we'd make selling flying rides to the kids?"

Stan stopped talking when a dinner plate sailed by his head and crashed against the kitchen wall. He didn't need both eyes to see that she hadn't warmed to the idea yet. God he was stupid.

She thrust something at him like a knights lance before a dragon. "Here's my credit card. Why don't you completely ruin us and buy some magic beans?"

"Honey, don't be like that - "

"Don't touch me. We said we were saving for a baby. A baby with you? God, I must have been mad."

Stan had always known that Alice had a temper. It was that raw fire within her that had first attracted him to her when a vending machine had stolen her money and she'd broken three knuckles pounding the hell out of it. But this was the first time that force of terrible strength had been turned toward him and he was scared. But she would see... once this flying carpet thing took off.

"The guy explained everything. Here, you lay it down like this."

"Get that thing out of my house. The wreckage of your face has warned me enough times of what you are. That this man's a fool."

"But we'll make a fortune, I'll show you."

"Don't you lay that ugly thing in my house!"

Stan picked the knot free and pocketed the rope. The carpet unfurled and he lay it down with great reverence like a priest before the altar. "It goes like this and -"

"Are you listening?" Alice screeched and hit him. She didn't realize she was holding anything until the table lamp cracked like an egg in her hand against his head and a raw flash of pain throbbed into her hand. Stan had been so sweet and concerned when she'd messed up her fist on that vending machine, bagging it with ice and kisses. Now he said nothing as he fell flat on his face, gave one wriggle like a landed fish and seemed to sleep.

Alice lost all sensation of noise when the broken bits of porcelain landed softly on the carpet beside the body.

"Stan? Stan!"

A quick inspection verified her suspicions. Mother had said she'd always had a temper but Alice didn't care. Stan had admitted a fondness for it, but now Stan wasn't speaking. He seemed quite dead.

Phone, she thought. Get an ambulance.

But instead of forcing her unsteady legs into an upright position to carry her across the room - across that damned carpet - toward the phone, she thought of a judge donning a black cap. A body going through a gallows trap door.

It was an accident, sir.

They would look at her record. Those 10 offences of fist fights in pubs would return and haunt her. The jury would accept she was a bad one and realize no other possible sentence. Liking her neck unbroken, Alice quickly set her mind in order.

There would be much to do before she could sleep soundly in the dawn.

No one came to Millers cliff. Not since the pirate days when highwaymen and villains used this place to divide up their loot taken from the recent dead. Children would admit to seeing the firelight from which they worked at night until mothers snapped their curtains shut and resisted their existence.

This was a bad place, but ideal for Alice's purpose. She stopped the car close to the cliff and hurt her hand again, catching it in the door as she started dragging the rolled up carpet out of the boot. It had made a handy body-bag. She would not have kept it even if it hadn't been bloodied. All evidence had to go into the sea far below if she was to sleep safe again.

Even from up here, the waves crashing against the chalk white cliffs tossed stinging salt in her face like acid from a spurned lover. Gulls cawed angrily at this trespasser, sure she'd come for her eggs.

"Shut up," she moaned and felt the ground thud as Stan in his Persian printed cocoon slammed head first into the soft mud. "Sorry honey," she said and saw in the obese moonlight that she was leaving a thin furrow in the ground as she dragged Stan's body toward the cliff.

The carpet certainly felt 1,000 years old. It seemed to be coming apart like moth eaten curtains and any magic it might have contained had surely melted away long ago.

"You always made life difficult," Alice hissed, out of breath when she reached the edge and prepared herself for a final shove. The sign said tourists with cameras should not come this close to the unstable edge, bits were falling off all the time but it had to look like an accident.

Of course she'd tell the police that Stan had suggested a romantic moonlit walk as that's what all slushy magazines said in love couples did. Another thing that Alice would insist she was, against their friend's opinion.

"Over you go," she said, and then hesitated. Would the carpet remain on him in the bouncing brine or would it be tossed aside and lost in the spray? She couldn't take the risk.

So your husband was taking a romantic walk whilst rolled up a carpet, huh?

Carefully, Alice started to unroll Stan's body out of the carpet like an unwanted sandwich filler.

"Don't forget the rope in his pocket," Alice told herself. Her mind was working too fast. There was so many things that could wrong, she had to slow down. To think this thing out completely.

"What rope?" Stan asked and tried to open his eyes, drunkenly.

He was about to ask what they were doing outside when Alice screamed as the wind picked up, filling the carpet outstretched in her hands like a sail. She stumbled, shocked by Stan's resurrection and only half formed the idea that he'd been stunned after all before the howling wind gave a final terrible blow and the carpet dragged Alice over the edge like a mangled kite.

The gulls lost their scream and all star light seemed to vanish as Alice tumbled down toward the quickly coming ground. She was sure she screamed as her mouth worked, but no sound came out.

Magic carpet, she thought hysterically like a drowning man would hold onto the nearest thing. Maybe it would offer some buoyancy. Maybe it would cushion the blow of impact.

God, I'm going to die, she thought but when she closed her eyes, the sickening crunch of impact didn't come.

The moonlight was still cold. The spray of the sea still cut into her face like tiny needles so if she felt something... she had to be alive? Not wishing to open her eyes and admit reality -- that she was indeed dead, slowly and then with more confidence, she snapped awake and found she was floating several feet above the crashing, angry sea.

She weighed nothing. At first, she thought she was floating, and then realized she was hovering like a bird above a dying meal.

"A flying carpet," she thought she said but only when she broke into wild uncontrollable laughter did she realize that she'd lost her last fragment of sanity and wished the sea had taken her after all.

Inspired By

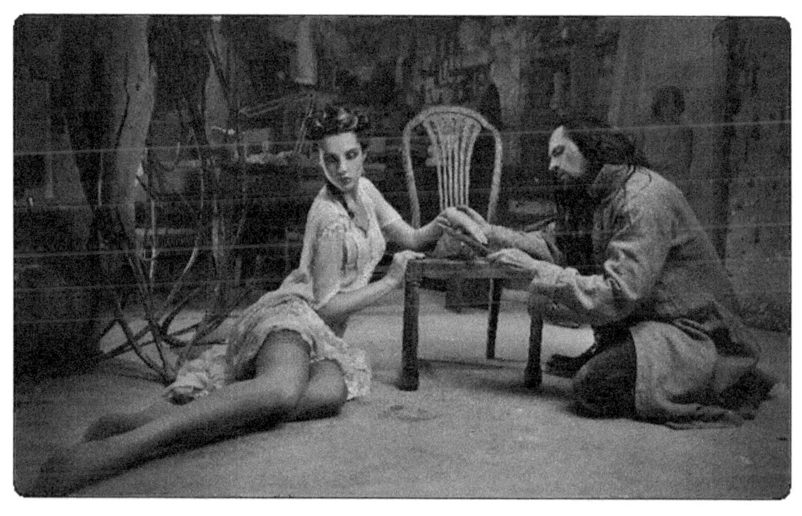

Beauty and the Beast

Beauty Before Us

By John Vicary

Mary visits town once a month. Sometimes in the winter she can make it as long as six weeks before she needs to don her wooden clogs and make the long trek down the winding dirt road for supplies. A few years ago it had been more often, but now she has some goats and a whole flock of chickens to keep her in dairy and eggs. She has learned enough to keep away for as long as possible; she doesn't know if she dreads the monthly visit more or if her neighbors do. Either way, it must be done.

Today is the day.

The walk isn't bad. Mary has always enjoyed a hearty constitution. It had served her well during her youth, when her sisters were often ill and she was left to nurse them. She had always managed to dodge the worst of the fevers that seemed the plague the others, and later she was thankful of her relentless good health when she moved into the Manor House with Lucien. It was an enormous place, and as such often given to drafts. Of course he didn't mind, he tended to complain of the heat, but she worried that no doctor would come to them if there was need. Not that she blamed the locals for their superstitions.

Before she knew better, she had heard strange tales of the Manor House. They all had. She had heard stranger tales of Lucien himself, but the truth had turned out to be as delicate as a spun sugar trifle, while the stories were far darker, as stories often are. Mary shakes her head to clear out the remembered pain of their first meeting, the long days of misunderstandings and the tears that had followed. They had both been so young and alone. Had the love that followed been destiny or just the course of nature? She has often wondered in the lonely years since.

The path to town curves through a forest, and Mary relaxes and forgets her dark thoughts of the past. This is her favorite part of the journey. She watches the interplay of shadow on the path and listens to the birdsong as she walks. Lucien used to be able to identify every call, but Mary knows only a handful. She hears a little bird chirping out of sight, but she cannot identify it from the few rising notes of its mating song. It reminds her of Lucien—as everything eventually seems to—and she quickens her steps. The village is just ahead.

The smell reaches her before the first house comes into view. Mary has grown used to the clean country air; the foul odors of town life are always a shock when she rounds the bend, and she struggles not to gag. It would not stand her in good stead to be sick in front of her neighbors. Not that it would make matters much worse. Mary grits her teeth and sets a course for the apothecary.

The streets are not crowded, but there are enough people about to begin the gossip. Mary keeps her head down in hopes that she will not be recognized until after her first stop, but she hears the overlapping whispers follow her like a stray dog in search of a free meal.

"… alone in that house…"

"… that monster…"

"I thought her husband had perished. If you could call him a husband. Not that any decent priest would ever marry them …"

"… say there is a child, but I've never seen one."

"She's plain crazy, I tell you! Always has been, always will be."

"… a witch…"

"… hasn't been right since that business with her father…"

"It roams at night, with red eyes. It's a hairy beast and she suckles it at her own breast. I've seen it with my own eyes!"

The urge to raise her hands to her ears and to scream is strong, but Mary bites the inside of her cheek and keeps her head high. The taste of blood floods her mouth, but she doesn't look back. "Almost there," she tells herself, then her hand is on the knob of the apothecary and she is inside the shop at last.

It is a dubious haven. Mr. Cross, the apothecary, is cordial enough but there are already other customers even this early in the day. Mary takes her place in line.

Mrs. Mahler sniffs. "I do believe I detect the nauseating odor of unwashed vermin just now."

"Indeed," Mrs. Power replies. She rummages in her handbag for a scented linen square with which to dab at her nose. "Quite powerful."

"Yoo-hoo! Mr. Cross!" Mrs. Mahler waves her hand. "You really must do something about the … lesser element. You don't want to allow just any old thing to wander in off the street, do you?"

Mrs. Power nods. "Think of your reputation."

Mr. Cross looks up from behind the counter, where he is measuring a draught into a bottle. He sees Mary and goes back to his work. "I'll be with you shortly, ladies. I do appreciate your patience."

"Hmph!" Mrs. Mahler pats her bun and Mary tries not to notice the women, but the shop is small and their words are loud in the enclosed space. "Did I tell you, Abigail, that I'm hosting a tea with Prunella Kemp next week?"

Mary stiffens. There is only one Prunella in the county, and it's her sister. Kemp must be her married name. Mary wrings her hands, desperate to hear news of her family.

"You don't say." Mrs. Power's voice is muffled from behind the pocket square.

"Yes. She's bringing her daughter and we're deciding on which fabric we're going to use in the town hall banners for next year's May Day celebration," Mrs. Mahler says.

Daughter… Mary's eyes fill with tears as she tries to imagine Prunella a mother. She has missed so much over the years.

"Mrs. Kemp recovered her figure so quickly after the baby, didn't she? Oh, I envy her. She always was such a beauty," Mrs. Power says. "Not like some."

"No, indeed. Not like some."

The words register and Mary realizes that both women are staring at her. She blushes and drops her gaze.

"Ladies! How may I be of service?" Mr. Cross has finished his work and steps forward to help the spiteful women, leaving Mary to her own thoughts.

Such a beauty… Beauty…

Mary remembers when she answered to that very name. That had been back when days were as bright as they were ever likely to be for her. Lucien was still alive and she believed that love was a strong enough shield to protect against any barb, no matter how sharp. Mary twists the iron band on her finger. It has grown large on her hand since Lucien has died, and she knows now that love is no match for the ravages of time. She sighs.

"Miss Little?"

Mary clenches her fists. Mr. Cross is kind, but he insists on addressing her by her maiden name. She steps to the counter. "The same supplies as always."

"Of course." Mr. Cross bags her standing order, the things she cannot provide for herself by living off the land.

Mary leans closer. "Also, I was wondering if you had looking into the medicine I had inquired about a few months ago."

Mr. Cross blinks behind his spectacles. "The hair loss solution? But I heard your husband … I mean, Lucien … what I mean to say is, Miss Little … " Mr. Cross stammers and begins again. "I apologize. This is most irregular. I was under the impression that the solution was … unnecessary now. Considering your circumstances. For which you have my sympathies, of course."

"Of course." Mary swallows the bitterness that rises like bile in her throat. "It's true, my husband did pass away. He wasn't a … beast. I know what people say. It isn't true." She's never said this out loud before, but it suddenly seems important to tell someone, anyone, and Mr. Cross is as good an audience as she is likely to have.

Mr. Cross looks around the store, but they are alone. "Oh, Miss Little, I never meant to imply—"

"It's Mrs. Gallagher, actually," Mary says. The words are flowing from a broken dam, and now that she is talking she can't seem to stop. "Lucien was a good man. He wasn't a monster. He just had this overgrowth of hair. That's all it was. Just hair, like your beard, like anyone has. That was all it was. That's all it ever was." Then she's finished, as if the well had run dry.

Mr. Cross is staring at her. "I understand, Miss L— Mrs. Gallagher. I had no idea. I've heard of such a condition. There's a name for it, in fact. It's called hirsutism."

"Hirsutism?" Mary repeats.

Mr. Cross nods. "Indeed. That's the medical word for it. It's very rare, of course, but I'm afraid that even if I were able to procure the medicines you asked for, it would not have helped your … husband. I'm not a doctor, mind you, but I am certain that his condition was caused by other internal factors that were much more complicated and beyond our understanding. Simply removing the hair from him would not have helped solve anything. Whatever caused his condition most likely contributed to his death. I'm sorry."

The room tilts around Mary. "But did you try to locate a hair loss serum? Do they exist?"

Mr. Cross frowns. "Mrs. Gallagher, I don't believe you comprehend what I have explained to you. It would not have helped."

"It would help some things!" Mary shouts. She forces herself to breathe until the ache clears from her throat and she can speak without strain. "I have—we have—a daughter."

Mr. Cross takes a step back from her, as if this news is contagious.

The door to the shop opens and a man enters. "Hello, old chap! I was wondering if you had my pomade in yet?"

Mr. Cross hasn't stopped staring at Mary. "I'll be with you in a moment, Mr. Chadwick." To Mary, he says, "There's nothing. I'm sorry, Mrs. Gallagher. I'm so very sorry for your troubles."

Mary opens her purse and gives him his money. She takes her bag of sundries and turns to exit the shop. She doesn't want to come back again, but she knows the time will come all too soon when she will need to.

As she reaches the door, Mr. Cross calls to her. "What is her name?"

Mary hesitates. "Belle," she says without turning. "It means beautiful in another language." She leaves before she can hear his answer.

On the way home it rains. Mary keeps her head down and watches her own feet take each step closer to where her daughter is waiting for her. She doesn't hear a single birdsong the whole way home.

Contributors

Darlena Cunha

Darlena Cunha is a former television producer turned freelance journalist and mom. She blogs daily at http://parentwin. com, and writes for Time Magazine, The Washington Post, The Atlantic and The Gainesville Sun, amid others. She's been published in McSweeney's, Wired, The Feminist Wire, and Offbeat Families plus many more.

Allison Hadley

Allison has a Bachelor of Arts degree in Film and Video Production and currently resides in the northwestern outreaches of the Chicagoland area. When she's not writing or dreaming, she can be found knitting, shooting pool, working on puzzles or doing archery.

Kate Harrad

Kate Harrad is a London-based writer. She blogs under the name Fausterella, which is also the title of her short story collection. Her first novel *All Lies and Jest*, a gently speculative thriller almost featuring vampires, was published by Ghostwoods Books in 2011.

Photo by Sandratei

Katherine Hannula Hill

Katherine Hannula Hill is a short story author, translator, and a contributing editor of Spirit Magazine. Born and raised in and around Seattle, Katherine has bounced from coast to coast, and country to country, moving from Boston to Grenoble, France to Madrid, Spain, and then to San Francisco. After double-majoring in French and Hispanic language and literature at Boston University, she lived and taught in A Coruña, Spain. She currently lives in New York where she uses her fluency in Spanish to advocate for victims of domestic violence and children in foster care.

David W. Landrum

David W. Landrum teaches Literature at Grand Valley State University in Allendale, Michigan. His short fiction has appeared in numerous journals and magazines. His novellas, *The Gallery*, *Strange Brew*, *and The Prophetess*, as well as his full-length novel, *The Sorceress of the Northern Seas*, are available through Amazon.

Kathleen Murphey

Kathleen Murphey teaches English Department courses and Women in History at Community College of Philadelphia. She has a master's degree and a Ph.D. in American Civilization from the University of Pennsylvania. She has looked at representations of female sexuality in popular literature for the past five years and presented papers on that topic at various conferences. Noting the absence of truly empowered representations of female sexuality in popular fiction, she has experimented with writing such representations. *Ruby and Romulus* is one such experimentation. She is married and the mother of three girls, 10, 12, and 14.

Rhema Sayers

Rhema Sayers is a retired physician, having given up medicine two years ago. She spent most of her career in emergency departments and loved what she did. To fill the huge void in her life, she has taken up writing, something she always wanted to do and has had some success with three stories published so far. Rhema now live in the desert in Arizona with three dogs and one husband (same one for decades). They adopted three little girls from China in the late 90's, but they are grown and living their own lives now.

John Vicary

John Vicary began publishing poetry in the fifth grade and has been writing ever since. A contributor to many compendiums, his most recent credentials include short fiction in the collections "Midnight Circus", "We Were Heroes" and "Temporary Skeletons". John is the Submissions Editor at Bedlam Publishing. He enjoys playing piano and lives in rural Michigan with his family. You can read more of his work at keppiehed.com.

Donald Weir

Donald Weir lives in Utah with his wife and son. He has a bachelor's degree from Arizona State University in creative writing.

Evelyn Wilbur

Evelyn Wilbur is a fan of creativity and giggles. What more can you ask out of life? Born and raised in West Covina, CA to supportive yet not all that creative parents, she often wondered if it wasn't for their shock and awe in her artistic abilities if she would have been less motivated to show them what she could do. She never grew tired of hearing her mother say, "I could never do that." She knew creativity was her happy place but it wasn't until she met her husband Bill in a writing program that her talents truly blossomed. He's more than just a mentor in writing and photography; he's also her best friend.

Matthew Wilson

Matthew Wilson has had over 150 appearances in such places as Horror Zine, Star*Line, Spellbound, Illumen, Apokrupha Press, Hazardous Press, Gaslight Press, Sorcerers Signal and many more. He is currently editing his first novel.